Praise for **WORKING IT OFF IN LABOR COUNTY**

"There's a country song on every page. . . . These characters want out, want in, yearn for some luck, lose whatever fortunes appear in their lives. This collection's a keeper, worthy of shelf space between Larry Brown and Merle Haggard."

—George Singleton, author of *You Want More: Selected Stories*

"Energetic, humorous, and full of heart. Thacker's voice feels fresh and alive."

—Jonathan Corcoran, author of *The Rope Swing*

"Thacker's linked collection is a carnival ride of southern gothic tales and freak-show oddities. . . . Hilarious, yes, but it's also a thoughtful exploration of the residents of Labor County, Kentucky, who are desperate to pull meaning out of loss."

—Marie Manilla, author of *The Patron Saint of Ugly*

"Larry Thacker's stories have bark, but they also have bite. These Labor County people aren't real, I keep telling myself that. They are just figments a writer made up in his head. But when you come away from this book, you'll feel that you've encountered a cast of characters who are going to stay with you—like newfound kin or a bad feeling in the bottom of your brain. Thacker writes like a wild man with a mean streak, breaking your tired heart all along the way."

—Charles Dodd White, author of *How Fire Runs* and *In the House of Wilderness*

WORKING IT OFF IN LABOR COUNTY

Stories

Larry D. Thacker

WEST VIRGINIA UNIVERSITY PRESS

MORGANTOWN

ISBN 978-1-949199-59-8 (paperback) / 978-1-949199-60-4 (ebook)

Library of Congress Cataloging-in-Publication Data
Names: Thacker, Larry, author.
Title: Working it off in Labor County : stories / Larry D Thacker.
Description: First edition. | Morgantown : West Virginia University Press, 2021.
Identifiers: LCCN 2020045760 | ISBN 9781949199598 (paperback) | ISBN
9781949199604 (ebook)
Subjects: LCGFT: Short stories.
Classification: LCC PS3620.H328 W67 2021 | DDC 813/.6—dc23
LC record available at https://lccn.loc.gov/2020045760

Book design, cover design, and photograph
by Than Saffel / WVU Press

For the many
who keep trying
to go home,
and the too few
who know
when they've arrived.

*I'm often reminded of what Uncle Archie would say
when I was asking too many questions:
"There's things about the world we don't know, boy.
Things seen. Some unseen.
We have to live amongst them all."*

Contents

Acknowledgments

My wife, Karin, will never know how much I appreciate her. She's never once doubted me along the way and filled me with more confidence than I'm worth. Anything I've managed has her fingerprints all over it. Ten pounds' worth of thank you stuffed in a five-pound bag to anyone touching the process of getting this story collection boosted into the realm of reality. Thanks to my blood family, mother, who passed before this collection became a reality, father, and sister (and Papaw Marsee, RIP), and my extended tribe family, AKA the students, faculty, and staff of the West Virginia Wesleyan College MFA in creative writing program. My East Tennessee home, Johnson City, Tennessee (y'all come visit). My roots home, Middlesboro, in southeast Kentucky, right near the Cumberland Gap. Abby Freeland and Charlotte Vester at West Virginia University Press. George Singleton, Marie Manilla, Jonathan Corcoran, and Charles Dodd White for their good words. Some of these stories originally appeared in slightly different or exact versions in the following publications. I thank those editors and other tireless staff: "Hot Ticket," *Fried Chicken and Coffee*, February 2016; "Day of the Dead Diner, Home of Juan D's Best

BBQ," *Vandalia Journal*, Summer 2017; "The Hard Thing," *Cowboy Jamboree: Harry Crews Tribute Issue*, 2017, *Cowboy Jamboree*, Pushcart Prize Nomination, 2017; "Benny and the Hill's Angels," *Pikeville Review*, 2019; "Hollow of the Dolls," *Grotesque Quarterly*, October 2017; "The Clown Brothers Eller," *Story and Grit*, 2018; and "The New Exhilarist," *Better Than Starbucks*, November 2016.

Working It Off
in Labor County

That's Constable Carp yelling for us to watch for idiot drivers.

It's a bad stretch of road through here for sure. In fact, an awful wreck killed two kids not long ago. Burnt them up. It's a well-known spot now, right up there where our work crew's headed, to those flat charred rocks. See? Where the flowers and stuffed animals pile up like a memorial.

Let's hope these vests the jailer gave us on the work bus do the trick and keep us from a similar demise. I'm guilty, but my offenses don't deserve the death penalty by a distracted driver. It's not like I robbed a bank and killed someone. It wasn't a bank I robbed, thank you very much. And no one died.

"Giving back" is slow going. I'm only halfway through. A hundred hours of community service sure does drag on, and the worst is yet to come with the weather. They say the rest of summer might hit record highs. It figures I'd end up out in the heat of the year working. I have brilliant timing.

This "service" is more about thinking than service, I'm convinced. It's like the county's just rubbing it in, designed to constantly remind me how I went from having a great faculty position at the college to cleaning up along the roads in front of the same school in a year's time. What a fall from the heights of academia, eh?

I've wondered if anyone keeps up with such interesting social plummets from grace because that sounds like a record. Maybe whoever publishes the *Busted in the Mountains* mug-shot trade paper might know. I looked and looked, but I never found my picture in it after the police ran me down. Ever wonder why everyone in that paper grins? Like they know something we don't. You'd think they'd be upset getting arrested for their fifth DUI. By that point it's just embarrassing.

But cleaning up roadsides isn't all that bad a gig. We're not that unlike a group of turkey vultures loitering on a thermal to swoop down and clean up behind messy people. That's called a *wake*. A collective of vultures. Odd since that's sort of what it looks like when they stand around pecking on a dead piece of meat.

We take care of the occasional festival recovery. Tent revival. Ever wonder why people insist on stuffing an illogical amount of discarded personal effects into an already overflowing garbage can? They sometimes take us out to pitch in on illegal dump cleanups. We helped with one last month out on the Powelton River. A really beautiful place. All but this thirty-foot-deep pit of junk sticking out like a sore thumb on the riverbank. Ever wonder why a person would pull off by a river with a truck of trash intent on tossing it down the bank, and something about the river's beauty, maybe the sound of the water on the rocks, the birds, anything, not stop them from ruining that spot? There was a bend in the river not too far downstream. Looked like a grandfather and his grandson were fishing. That place was special to them, I imagined, and there we were waist deep in rusting refrigerators and rotting diapers.

Yet there are worse ways of working off a debt to society, aren't there? Like behind bars, which I only dodged by the hair of my eye teeth.

Life was different not very long ago. I was a professor of history at Middlegate Community College. Eight years I'd been there. My specialty was the American Civil War. Loved it. Loved my students. Loved the school. I was happy.

I was a nut for history. I'm not so sure anymore. It seems dear Clio, the Greek goddess muse of history, played me for a fool. I used to keep a picture of her on my office wall. The old girl's only laughing at me now, though. Her and my ex, Clara. Yep, Clara and Clio, given up on me, though the ex hinted we might reconcile after I've fulfilled my debt to society.

Now hear me out before you assume I'm just another felon who claims he's innocent. I'm not.

I'd served two years of a three-year appointment on the Labor County History Society board of directors when I had a falling out with some of the leadership.

That was a shame. I enjoyed having a hand in Labortown's historical preservation. This is my home after all. As the only son of the seventh generation of McMichelsons from Labor County, I've always felt like I had a duty to take up for our little part of the mountains. If we didn't do it, who would? It seems like everybody but people from here are sure about what we're about, and they make money being wrong about it.

The old Dillard Memorial City Jail houses the museum, which makes for an interesting setup of cell-to-cell displays, especially with the cell-bar doors intact. Each room represents a different stage in the timeline of Labor County history, often with mannequins dressed in period fashions performing activities of the time. The museum was always sending volunteers to auctions to bid on lots from stores that flopped. That's the best way to get cheap dummies.

Cell #1: Pre-Columbian Kentucky. The stone walls were painted to resemble our steep wooded mountains, from back when Kentucky was known as the "Dark and Bloody Ground," and in the middle of the room were two bare-chested, makeup-smeared Cherokees eating by a fake fire.

Cell #2: Frontier settlement. The walls were painted like the insides of a fort. In the middle of the room sat a long hunter clad in leather and pelts and a frontier woman sitting and eating by a fake fire.

Cell #3: Labortown established, 1873. The walls were painted like the inside of a cabin and in the middle of the room was a farmer, his wife, and two kids sitting and eating by the fake fire of a hearth.

Cell #4: You get the picture.

We'd experienced some petty crime at the museum. Preserving history isn't easy when chunks up and go missing. It couldn't be helped with well-meaning, but unorganized volunteers. The occasional pack of postcards vanished. Bookmarks. An irreplaceable antique yearbook from the library. But when a tenth annual Labor Days (get it? Labor County?) ashtray went missing, that was the last straw as far as I was concerned.

At the next quarterly meeting I brought up, in the form of a proper motion, the idea of installing security cameras. It got a second. We fought for an hour over that idea. But when it came time to voting on actually passing the idea of purchasing a three-camera system (with monitor), which required three out of five to pass majority, the chairwoman, Teretha, who usually didn't vote unless it was a tie (and wouldn't have then if she didn't have to), gave a long speech about how it would send the wrong message to the community, and what would we do if we accused the wrong person, and what would our procedures be, etc., etc.

I'd done my homework. I had answers for all her concerns.

Of course, everyone knew why she was muddying the waters. Her husband, Kurt, is the town pet kleptomaniac. He's been ripping off the museum for years. When I came on board everyone was used to turning a blind eye. Maybe they thought it was quaint. Maybe they didn't have the proof they needed. Maybe they dreaded the argument.

I personally didn't think it was so cute. Especially after I'd loaned my Civil War collection to the museum. I'd spent years collecting that stuff. I had a Union three-band Enfield rifle, with bayonet. Most of a Union officer's uniform, minus the left arm of the coat and shirt supposedly ripped off by a cannonball, blood stains intact. A journal kept by Oliver "Ollie" Howerton, one of the town founders who survived the war and went on to be Labor County's most successful hog farmer in the 1870s. Not to mention a bunch of small items like squashed lead bullets and chunks of metal dug up from battlefields.

The best piece of the collection, though, was a portion of a battlefield oak tree trunk. Six feet tall and full of bullets and solid cannon shot. The damage of the battle hadn't killed the tree, so some of the iron balls were partially grown over, as if the tree was slowly swallowing up the foreign objects. It was a fine collection. They'd even put it all in a corner on its own and called it *The McMichelson Collection*. I admit I was proud of the little fake brass label.

I told them I thought the decision to not heighten security was terribly unprofessional.

Teretha said I could quit my time on the board early if I felt uncomfortable with the decisions arrived at so very democratically by the esteemed board.

I told her she could kiss my socialist ass.

I should have stayed on and done my best to make the rest of my time on the board as miserable an experience for them as I could, though I liked most of them, but I figured I had better things to do, so I huffed off with the promise of returning for my property. It was very dramatic.

That was a mistake. One that eventually led to my standing here picking up soggy cigarette boxes on the dangerous shoulder of Route 17.

I never was a litterer. Who does this? Trash flies off the backs of trucks. That I understand. People make mistakes. But the things we pick up out here? The beer cans. Is there that much drinking and driving? The fast-food junk. Sure, damage the earth while you're scarfing down two double-cheeses, some fries, and a large milkshake. A whole bag of unwashed underwear (men's and women's)? Don't ask.

Anyway, after I cooled down for a few days, I returned to the museum. I was undressing a mannequin wearing my one-armed Union uniform when the volunteer on shift asked if she could help me. It was Janine. I'd known her for some years.

"Janine, it's me, Roger," I laughed.

"I'm sorry, sir, but I have to ask you not to interfere with the museum's historical displays."

"Janine, this stuff's mine. Remember?"

She pursed her lips and didn't answer. I could tell she was in a quandary. Then she walked off a few steps and made a frantic call on her cell. Probably to Teretha, I figured. I heard her whispering. I could hear the conspiratorial temper in her voice.

"Janine, I need the key to the cabinet to get my things," I interrupted.

"Teretha says to remind you how you gave those items to the historical society, sir."

Why was she calling me sir?

"On temporary loan," I corrected. "I never outright gave anything to anybody!" I could hear Teretha's voice yacking into Janine's ear with instructions. "And quit calling me *sir*, Janine. I've know you for how many years?"

"No, sir, Teretha insists. Those items were gifts, sir. She remembers you telling her so."

"I did no such damned thing!" I was pissed now. I turned and continued on my mission, but in a hurry now. I needed to be quick. But despite my speed I was still filling my boxes when the police got there. It's a small town. The station's only three doors down.

I argued my case, but without paperwork, which neither side of the argument had, the items would have to stay until something official was settled.

"It's my stuff! There's my name right there." I pointed to the fake brass plaque.

Officer Carl Banks and I went to high school together. "I see that. You can either work it out calmly or you can sue them, but you can't just walk out of here with it today, Roger," Officer Banks told me with no hint of wiggle room in his voice on the matter. He could tell what was going on, but only shook his head at the situation.

"It's a nice collection. Too bad, Roger," he said. "What else you been into lately?"

So I gave the calm route a try. The police couldn't help. I called the board members to lobby my side. They couldn't find any paperwork to help me out and they weren't making any more waves than necessary. They figured it would work itself out. Teretha had them steamrolled. For all I knew, Kurt had made off with the evidence. If they hoped I didn't have the money, or the patience, for letting a lawsuit work its magic, they were right. I appealed to the city commission. They refused to deal with it based on jurisdiction. I went to the chamber of commerce. Not their business. The town drunk's about the only one I didn't burden with my appeal for common sense.

The longer it drew out the angrier I got. Everyone that heard my story was on my side, but quietly. I admit I had hatred growing in my heart.

I went to see Preacher Ed. His new Church of the Holy Fire of God was only a block over from the museum. We went to high school together. I knew him long before he was a man of God, which was a fairly new venture for him, though pretty convincing.

He was trimming out a new baptistery when I walked in.

"I've heard about your predicament. They doing you wrong, man?"

"They are, Ed. They're stealing from me, no two ways about it."

I'm not a regular religious man, but I was raised Presbyterian. I think I was needing someone to talk me out of a terrible thing at that point. All sorts of bad ideas were crossing my mind.

"I'll get my belongings back. They're playing games with the wrong guy. I spent a lot of money and time putting that collection together and it ought to be where I say it should be."

"How you think you'll settle this up, Roger?"

"I'm hoping not to have to resort to anger, Ed," I told him, hoping for some good counsel.

His eyes brightened. "Lord. You thinking about torching the place, man?" I'd seen that look before.

"What? No! No. Hell no, of course not, Ed." Was he kidding?

"No, no . . . of course not," he agreed quickly, laughing off the joke. "You know me and hell-fire, right? Just making sure you weren't about to do anything too drastic. You want me to pray with you while you're here?"

Of course I wouldn't resort to such violence as arson. Why would I take a chance on burning up my own collection? That's plumb foolish.

My brilliant plan was to rob the place in broad daylight.

It was a Monday afternoon, three o'clock, the slowest day and hour for historical-society museum visiting, at least in Labor County. I'd done the math when I joined the board. I was hoping for a little cooperation from the volunteer that day, Burt Beverly, a retired history teacher from the local school system. I'd gone to high school with Burt's son, Burt Jr.

I knew Burt loved to talk, so my plan was to get him started. I walked in, yelled out my hello, which lured Burt out of the office. His face flushed a little when he saw me.

"Relax, Burt. Think of me like any other visitor, okay? How you been?"

We could talk for hours. Town history, the county, southeast Kentucky, how the Civil War divided this part of the country, the mine strikes, mine wars, mine tragedies, mine economic collapse, environmental destruction, the hog industry. UFOs. But Burt was an expert on local vice during prohibition and up during a resurgence in the fifties. He loved bragging to visitors how the most popular whorehouse for three counties was the old hotel right across the street, The Drifter. Drink. Gambling. Women. Shootouts. You name it, Burt was an expert.

"Fine. Fine. Not quite as fun with you gone, I might add," he offered in a kind of whisper. I did feel bad about what I was about to do.

I inquired about a cell display we'd worked on and he got really excited about how far he'd managed. "Just about got *The Roaring Fifties* finished up," he reported proudly. The walls were painted with bars and hotels that used to line Labor Avenue, this very street. The Drifter was nicely depicted with its two stories, the red brick facade, the Victorian style roof pitch. The partying silhouettes in certain positions in the windows gave a great effect.

He had a card game set up in the middle of the room with

dummies in three-piece suits playing cards, whiskey shots all around, a cocktail-sipping woman fancily dressed and eavesdropping over a player's shoulder, a bar in the back with a bartender.

"I ran out of room for anyone to be eating a meal," he said, sounding disappointed.

"Or a fireplace," I added.

Burt was on a tangent about gluing down the poker chips since he knew patrons would make off with them as souvenirs just as I shut the gated door on him and clipped a padlock into the hasp of the door.

The clang of the door startled him.

"Whoa! What are you doing?"

"I need to get my things, Burt. You'll understand, won't you?"

"Well, shit, I would have helped you, buddy. If you'd asked." That surprised me.

"I thank you for that, Burt, but I can't take any chances, as you can imagine."

Burt prided himself on being the last man in the county—at least the city—who hadn't given in to the pressure of buying a cell phone yet—not even a flip phone. I was glad of that now. He wouldn't call for help, even if reception did suck inside these stone walls.

"Well, just don't leave me in here all night. Thelma's making pork chops for supper."

I had it figured out. I locked the front door, turned the hanging sign to closed, and flipped most of the lights off. An effective out-to-lunch look. Maybe an obscure holiday.

I broke the lock off the display case with the bayonet tip from my Enfield rifle and bagged up "Ollie" Howerton's journal and my other small items.

That's when someone knocked at the door. There was muffled talking. Then flashing lights bouncing off the walls. Shit.

"Roger!" More knocking. Louder.

"Hey, Roger? You in there?"

I spied a glance at the front entrance. It was Officer Banks.

"Roger! Teretha gave us a call! Said you were down here about to cause a problem. Looks like we're too late, maybe?"

Now how would she have known?

I yelled back. "How's she know that, Carl?"

He was on the phone, with her apparently. Jeez. Did she ever do any dirty work face-to-face?

"She asks that you . . . smile for the cameras." I could tell he was trying not to laugh.

Cameras. Really? After all that rigmarole about not wanting them? After me quitting over it!

"Cameras? Are you kidding me? Where!"

"She said there's no tellin'."

I looked around as inconspicuously as I could. If there were cameras in the lobby where my display was located they weren't of the traditional design. They might be tiny pinhole cameras. I gave a slow look up to Ollie Howerton's five-by-four-foot oil painting hanging on the wall. It was to my right about ten feet away. I could just make out the color difference from one eye to the other. The idiots had punched out his right eye for the sake of a hidden camera. Was nothing sacred? Sorry, Ollie.

I yelled back to Burt. "Burt! Did you know about these cameras?"

"No, Roger, I didn't, or I would have been more adamant about you not doing this. I actually thought you were going to get away with it. Everyone knows it's your stuff."

I yelled up at the painting. "You hog-lovin' traitor!"

I scanned the lobby for other secret spots, trying to think like Teretha, as pained as that felt. I didn't suspect any other places. I stepped up on the donated pew from the old Martin's First Freewill Baptist Temple and eyed the camera close. Then I poked the town founder in the spy eye, effectively blinding Teretha. I hope she felt it all the way to the brain.

It was time to move. I dragged the Union uniform off the mannequin and slipped the wooly thing on. I admit I felt strange having one naked arm exposed with the undershirt and coat missing arms from that mythic cannonball wound. I yanked on the trousers and the leather boots and cap and left the sweaty Hawaiian shirt, Bermuda shorts, and flip-flops I'd worn in on the floor as a final heap of goodbye.

I clipped the bayonet on and slung the rifle over my shoulder. I was ready to go, but for one important item: the battlefield tree trunk. I didn't care if it weighed more than seventy pounds, I wasn't leaving this man on the field. I was more worried about hauling that monster out of the building than I was with how I was actually getting out of the building myself. I was cornered.

"Roger, stay calm and come on out. Let Burt go and we'll make this just about the stolen items. You'll probably avoid any kidnapping charges."

Kidnapping?

"Kidnapping?"

"Yeah, you're digging a deeper hole the longer you draw this out, buddy!"

Hoping I'd disabled the only hidden camera in the lobby, I peeped down the cell-block corridor.

"Burt, I'm throwing you the keys. Let yourself out and join me in the lobby if you want to help me out of this jam maybe. I sure as hell don't want a kidnapping charge on my head. You're my friend," I told him.

"That'd be pretty funny, wouldn't it?" he yelled, clanging around with the skeleton key.

"You're not sore for me locking you up?" I asked him, not a little paranoid he was poised to run straight for the front door.

"Naw. This is the most fun I've had since I started to volunteer."

He came around the corner and saw me.

"Now why am I not surprised you're dressed like the reenactment of Pickett's Charge?"

I tossed him my shirt, shorts, and shoes. He looked at me strangely.

"This is a Union uniform."

"Don't matter. You're fighting an uphill battle, I'd say."

"We're about the same height and build?"

"So."

A minute later and he was dressed like I was when I walked in, but not terribly happy about the fact.

"Buddy, these clothes stink a little."

"Hey, I was working hard. This is a crime after all."

He nodded, breathing through his mouth.

"Hopefully the last Teretha saw me by the camera I looked like you do now, so keep your head down. I'm parked out front. Make sure Carl sees you heading down the sidewalk. I only need a few seconds. Let's hope no one's watching the back loading door to see you heading out. If they are, we're screwed."

Burt was all for it. He ducked his head and went for the back door and I took a deep breath and hiked my battlefield tree trunk up on my right shoulder and prayed for all hell to break loose outside.

When I heard Officer Carl yell at "me" to "Stop right there!" I knew the game was afoot. I counted to ten and went for the front door and didn't see anyone on guard, unlocked it, and glanced up and down the street.

Burt was already a block away kind of walk-jogging and fixing to turn into a back alley with Carl in the squad car right behind him with the lights and siren going full blast. He was yelling at "me" over the intercom to "Hold it right there, Ronnie!" and to "Freeze!"

I took off down the steps of the museum, but the weight of the tree trunk buckled my right knee as I made it to the sidewalk. The best I could do, short of getting crushed by the thing and making a ruckus, was hoisting it up and away from me with all I was worth. Luckily, but sort of unluckily, the tree trunk bounced off the trunk of my car and stabbed through the back windshield, nesting an end neatly in my backseat, which was fine since that's where I was headed with the thing. I picked myself up, skinned knees and all, happy I hadn't impaled myself with my own bayonet, tossed the rifle through the back windshield as well since it was available now as an opening, hopped in, and took off.

My next move was to lay low. I admit I hadn't thought much past getting away with my goods. Truth be told, part of me was probably hoping to get shut down right there at the museum. At least I'd made my point. I guess.

I drove around awhile wondering what was next. Some criminal.

I remembered my cousin, Archie. He'd been digging a fallout bunker for years. Maybe he'd let me hide out there and figure out my next move. Knowing him, the bunker's accommodations would be as comfortable as a house, but come to find out he'd turned the whole property into some sort of roadside weirdness. I was explaining my predicament to him, pretty much begging for help, when a busload of grade schoolers showed up for an unscheduled tour. Apparently it was some obscure state holiday. I was forced to play along and gave a lecture on Civil War uniforms and signed autographs so as to not blow my cover, but before I could sound my personal retreat, one of the little squirts snapped a shot of me posing with my rifle and posted it on Facebook *and* Instagram. If I hadn't had to explain why I had an arm of my own when the uniform was missing a set of arms, I'd have gotten away. The delay cost me dearly. Carl and the other deputies had me blocked on both ends of Archie's road.

They charged me with felony theft. Could have gotten one to five years. Funny how an organization that couldn't find proof of my temporary donation was able to run down documentation of my collection's estimated value. Just enough value, in fact, to guarantee my crime qualified as a felony. In other words, I'm a felon for having stolen my own property. They didn't press anything related to kidnapping, thank goodness, and Burt wasn't charged with any sort of contributing to the mess.

I was given two years unsupervised probation and a hundred hours community service. I was fired from the college, prevented from coming to within five hundred feet of the museum via restraining order, and, as if Clio the Muse had been joy-sticking the whole fiasco for her own entertainment, I was ordered to give back my Civil War collection. My back windshield's still taped up with plastic.

Well, y'all, I'd love to stand here all day talking about all my screwups, but this ditch won't beautify itself. Besides, it's getting on around lunchtime and Constable Carp hinted that a sincere morning of work might result in the county picking up the tab for lunch down at Juan's BBQ. If you've ever had the pleasure of eating there before you can imagine my anxiousness to get this job done and done right. If you'll excuse me.

Hot Ticket

You could find Ed loafing around the Quik Pick #2 just about every Tuesday and Thursday close to four in the morning. He was an early one. He'd slow-sip coffee and flirt with Elma as much as she'd allow, all the while mindlessly shuffling through layers of tossed scratch tickets that accumulated all night in the garbage bins.

The only money he'd spend on the Lotto was from the rare winning ticket someone tossed by mistake. People would toss winning tickets sometimes. It was like hunting treasure. He resented a little not being able to afford his own, like some folks that sat around all day as if the store was a neighborhood casino, spending disability money on handfuls of dollar scratch tickets. He hardly fished out a winner, but he had found a fifty-dollar ticket once and was able to gorge on a big lunch at the Waffle Hut with enough left for three-gallon jugs of gasoline. Mostly they'd accumulate in his wallet.

Ed wasn't the only one scouring for tossed tickets, but he was one of the few with the patience for it. Some were awfully territorial. Sammy tore into the bin around seven in the morning on Mondays. John would get there about ten on Tuesdays and Wednesdays. It seemed like Alfred never left the building sometimes. You could see it in their eyes when they spotted a bunch in the garbage, swiveling their heads around like a hungry animal. Ed was more laid-back. It just helped pass the time before the sun was up and the grass dried.

He was sipping his second cup of coffee, half-awake one morning, watching Elma sweep up around the Coffee Oasis, when the huge flashy neon sign over the counter flipped from 499 to 500 million dollars on the Super Lucky Ball Cash Jackpot Sweepstakes. That wadded stash of winners in his wallet sprung to life. They vibrated they wanted out so bad.

He hurried over to the scratch counter, swept the little mounds of grey shavings away, and emptied his wallet of those tickets, flattened them out, organized them to be polite to Elma, and made his way to the checkout.

"Elma, I reckon it's time to spend these winners," he whispered, handing over the handful of ragged tickets.

She winked. "Feeling lucky, Ed?"

He cracked a grin. "You make me feel lucky, Elma. I wouldn't bother if you weren't working right now. That sign just changed to 500 million."

She looked up, blinked, and gave a sigh. "It sure did, didn't it? God, what I'd do for that kind of money."

"That sounds like a prayer," Ed offered as the little speaker set to yelling *Yahoo!* every time she scanned a ticket. "You won twenty-three dollars, honey. Not bad."

He perused the thickly bound rolls of scratch-offs secured behind Plexiglass along the counter and studied his cash.

"How many you want?"

"Let's do ten worth of Lucky Ball tickets. And seven dollars in gas." That left him three dollars. He eyed his favorite scratch-off, the "All Fired Up" 100,000-dollar golden ticket.

"And give me a number eight. I'm feeling *all fired up*, Elma."

She smiled, attuned to his subtle joke.

The sun inched up over the eastern ridge, finally raising the temperature, new light slow-chasing shadows across the pot-hole-cratered lot. Ed clinked open his silver Zippo with a mindless snap of his fingers and lit a smoke. Thumbed over the fading inscription of flames on the lighter, once brighter red and yellow. He was patient. He'd move when the light reached his back bicycle tire. This far back in the hills meant the sun was up later, meant the grass dried later.

With what was left of a second cigarette smoldering from is clamped lips, he filled two gas cans he'd balance-rigged over the back of his bicycle. He never worried about the fumes. He figured if he was bound to die in a fire that would have happened long ago.

A woman at another pump stared at the dangling cigarette as he pumped. He squinted back through the smoke's heat with a grimace matching hers.

"What?" he snapped.

Her eyes rounded, surprised.

"Well, if you can't wait to smoke until you've pumped your gas you must be an addict." She huffed and bolted toward the store, to tattle probably. He thought he could hear her say something about hoping he'd blow up.

"Honey, I'm addicted to more than smoking," he muttered with a pleasured grin. Then he peddled off to mow some yards, totting his mower alongside and whistling loud enough so Elma might could hear him heading down the road to start his day.

Ed accomplished more than mowing yards when he was working. He was scouting. People quietly knew the deal. You didn't acquire a reputation as Labor County's "go to" arsonist without good reason. Who couldn't put two and two together? Why would he be mowing at some long-abandoned property right before it went up in smoke? Or the caretaker of a slumlord dump that was so run-down not even the most desperate tenant would live there—that just happened to burn?

People knew. They just didn't give a damn.

Ed felt like he was offering a service. Homeowners liked it, especially if it helped them renovate. Insurance companies were more or less indifferent. They were charging people higher rates anyway because of the frequency of fires. They'd pay out and drop customers from coverage. Landlords liked it for the insurance payout. The slumlords loved it when a place burned, especially if one was barely up to code or they were getting pressured to condemn one and tear it down. State investigators were so backlogged with arsons across southeast of Kentucky they'd mostly given up on all but the fires that hurt or killed someone.

That was a rule Ed wouldn't break. Never hurt someone with a fire.

As for the fire departments, as long as no one was hurt, they were fine with having steady work and training. Wasn't it the purpose of firefighters to fight fire?

What little guilt Ed occasionally felt about his semisecret occupation was seldom long-lived. With so few caring and so many benefiting, there were days when being a fire bug felt like a regular job.

But most regular jobs don't run the risk of killing you.

Gasoline is a volatile, unpredictable son of a bitch of an incendiary. But it's cheap and it works. Fumes build up and that's what burns. Pour a thin line through a structure and wait long enough and when it ignites every window in the house blows out. He liked old carpeted places. Wood floors took too long to catch. Old curtains were good. Linoleum. And you couldn't just start a fire in one room, the whole structure had to catch. For a thousand dollars he guaranteed a fire so involved by the time the fire department arrived they'd just throw some water on it to keep it from spreading. A neat pile of charred splinters was what he wanted by the next morning. That kept him as arson's favored son. That and no arrests, of course.

Truth be told, though, he'd have done most of his jobs for free. Some ventured he had a fetish. Ed reckoned he did. Very little in the world excited Ed more than fire. There was such a mystic life about it. The violence. The risk. The pleasantly lit process of decay. The artful power of it all. The potentially deadly heat. It was a dance with a force of annihilation. Universal. Something physical morphing to no more than what a light wind might sweep away. An utter elemental disappearance. Magical. Dangerously beautiful. Addictive.

Poetic.

By late that night, Ed was rethinking this love affair with fire, though, dazed and on his back as greedy fingers of flames licked up the ceiling of the stairway he'd just flown backward through. Hadn't he done everything right? Scoped the property, estimated the inside before breaking in the back window. A gallon of gas would do the job.

Yet he hadn't counted on the several plastic milk jugs of old gas in the cellar. He'd set the fire down there first and was on his way out when the jugs instantly melted, spreading pools of fuel across the floor and blowing him out of the cellar stairway up into the kitchen. Now the fire was nearly on him, slow stalking, upside down, crawling across the blackening kitchen ceiling and catching the curtains of the back door and window he'd crawled through.

He tried shaking off the concussion, close to blacking out, smoke broiling the air above his head, singeing down on the tips of his ears and nose.

This is it. You're blacking out.

He rolled to his belly.

And burn.

Felt it nipping at his head and neck like hot breath.

And die.

He was always amazed how loud fire could be.

Horribly.

Then the voice was there.

You think you know me?

A figure, like a man, *but not*, emerged, the black above parting in a swirl to make way for his stature, his outline unclear. His raiment was smoke, peeling from his body, twirled with the living orange of heat, eyes in dark glowing knowledge.

Ed folded his hands, forcing up a gaze. The black was lit at the fringes with orange, living fire. He knew as surely as the pain stabbing him he was staring into a hell he'd seldom considered.

You think you know me?

It was the devil himself, wasn't it?

You don't know me. Not yet.

Tears from the smoke and heat streamed his cheeks.

"Don't wanna know you, you devil."

You're about to meet me.

Pain like red-heated numberless pincers clamped into him, bending him double. He was screaming for the Lord then, his voice a squeak under the crackling consumption of the vanishing world. Had he ever done such a thing? Meant it. Desperately called out to God?

Then another voice was there. The smoke peeled back in swirls. A cabinet fell from the wall and exploded smoking fragments across the room.

You don't know me, do you?

"No Lord . . . I don't . . ."

You want to die here? So horribly?

"No," he gagged, nearly puking out the meek words.

Swallowed up in a forever hell worse than this?

"No!"

What do you want to happen?

"I want to live, Lord! Live!"

Another explosion fired off in the cellar, pushing more black over his back. The room darkened. Everything roared.

"Let me live . . . I'll do anything . . . don't let me burn, Lord! Anything."

Anything? "Yes."

You might wish you hadn't made this deal.

There was a groan and crash and his back was showered in hot glass. His sleeves were smoking. His mind snapped back clearer. The curtains had burnt up and nearby window glass was buckling and falling in, a rush of night air slicing into his smoke-packed lungs like ice picks. There were sirens. He hobbled out, the shirt on his back smoking, the stink of his own cooked hair all over him. He heard laughter as he stumbled up the back hill into the safety of the forest, half-blind and barely pulling air into his body.

He was hacking up black chunks all night, shivered with fever from pockmark burns on his arms, neck, and head, down his back. He drank so much water his belly swelled round and felt like it might split open. He'd toss and turn, get up, pace. Groaned and winced. Getting caught wasn't his worry. But the voices. The voices relayed in his mind, tearing him away from the idea of sleep when he finally closed his eyes. The red of fire never went away. Was that God? Was that the devil? What craziness was this? How was he supposed to recognize God, Jesus, Satan? Any of them?

He went to the kitchen to force some food into his nauseous and bloated belly. His singed, nasty jeans and shirt were pooled in the floor where he'd dropped them. His wallet was laying there on the top of the sodden mess, the orange-peach corners of his Lucky Ball tickets sticking from the worn leather folds. Ed grinned, a funny surge of fantasized relief flooding his imagination. He found a penny in the floor and started scraping.

Golden Ticket numbers: 13. 43. 24.

    12. 17. 34

    43. Free Ticket. 35.

    A free ticket. *Better than nothing.*

    13. 32. 26.

    Thirteen?

Ed chuckled and scratched under the number, hoping for maybe a dollar. Then his fingers stopped moving and he batted his dry eyes in the kitchen's puny light.

Under the number thirteen was *$100,000* in fat golden letters.

" . . . and when you smash the red-hot gates of hell open, soul first, and feel that dreaded condemnation, in spirit and body, you will grieve the days you turned from the grace of God's gift! You'll know in your heart, as you rot in a devil's hell for eternity, you turned away, brothers and sisters!"

The congregation responded.

Amen . . . Glory! Amen.

"I was there . . . turning my greedy, deaf ears from God's voice. Knowing God's message was in my ear every day, around every corner, judging my every bad choice. But I heard him, finally, in my time of need, and almost too late. I heard God and now I stand today preaching my promise to him!"

Amen. Amen.

"I was broke—like many of you."

Amen.

"I was sad and lonely . . . just plain tired of living. Like some of you, maybe, here this morning."

Amen. Bless him, Lord!

"I was burdened with evil. Not living for God!"

Amen!

"Now here we are, blessed with hope, free from hell and Satan's mighty and stubborn grip on this here old, tired Earth."

Ed paused. Took a deep breath. Dabbed sweat from his brow with his shirt sleeve. They were listening. They were all listening.

Three months had passed since Ed had won the Golden Ticket jackpot, his world instantly turned inside out. Upside down. God had obviously intervened, hearing his desperation, setting his path anew. That was the easy part, the winning. The salvation. But then the hard part kicked in, the not making a fool of God for letting him escape that pit of hell-house that was burning down around his head.

"Broke in my pocket and broke of spirit in the morning—a small fortune in my pocket from the mighty hand of the living God by sundown!" he'd witness to anyone that listened. "The ways of God are not mysterious to those who believe in miracles."

He'd opted for the one-time payout. Seventy-three-thousand dollars. The Thursday morning the state transferred the funds he had $13.56 in his checking account. Like magic, by noon there was $73,013.56. Everyone stared at him at the bank, a mix of grins and frowns, all judging in some way or another.

"What do you plan on doing with all that money, Ed?" a cashier who'd never paid him any attention flirted as she flipped down a thousand dollars in hundreds. He liked the way she licked her thumb every three bills. Funny how he was suddenly more attractive.

"The Lord's work," he mumbled without thinking. Not a great

way to flirt back, he guessed. But it was the truth, wasn't it? He was contracted now by the spirit. "Maybe a new lawnmower," he joked, to keep it lighthearted.

"You all know I've been on the wrong side of the law some. That ain't no big secret."

He hesitated for effect.

"But who among you ain't been?"

Bless him, Lord. True that!

"We've all fallen short of God's grace. But to be blessed with epiphany! You all know what an epiphany is? It's a sudden realization. Like a shot of lightning to the brain, brother! I won't bother y'all with the details, but let's just say I was into things I ought not to have been. And it about killed me."

Bless him.

"Then the voice of God Almighty came down and wrung me up by the shirt collar and showed me hell . . ."

Lordy!

Ed's stinging sweat filled eyes scanned the crowd. It had doubled in the last month, filling the pews he'd bought from that failed Mount Vernon Holiness Church. Now the pews were near full and the store front rental he'd leased was feeling near cramped.

The morning's preaching felt good. That is, until Dillon Hamby magically appeared on the back row. He'd snuck in. If Dillon was there it wasn't for the preaching. He'd be bringing work. Work Ed couldn't do anymore. Work he wouldn't do, by God.

A noticeable stumble worked its way into Ed's train of thought as he avoided Dillon's eyes.

"Let us pray," he abruptly offered the flock.

He heard the quiet talk as everyone milled about, hugging and handshaking and sipping coffee after the service.

"Nobody can preach hell-fire and brimstone like Ed."

"I start sweatin' when he talks burnin' in hell like that. It scares me."

"Well, he ought to know fire, now shouldn't he?" another whispered.

Ed avoided Dillon and started cleaning up the donut crumbs and coffee spills. Dillon waited. Ed could feel him in the room, sensed the shallow wheeze from the man's six-foot, three-hundred-pound frame. Dillon dabbled in lots of things besides slum-lording, which is how he'd met Ed in the first place. He was also the part-time high school offensive line coach and part-time operator at the water treatment plant.

"Got a job for ya, Ed," Dillon finally offered, sure he already knew Ed's answer.

"It's good to see you, too, Dillon," Ed lied.

"I said I got work for you."

Ed huffed and glanced up from wiping down the coffee maker. This conversation was bound to happen eventually.

"Dillon, you know I'm preaching now. I'm done with that. All of it. I told you that on the phone. I gotta be done."

Dillon smirked with a grunt. "Yea, but I wanted to see for myself. I tell ya, though, the Lord done good pickin' you to preach hell, huh?" he laughed. "You almost convinced me." It's a good scam though. How much you rakin' in when you pass them plates?"

"I mean every word of it."

"Maybe. Maybe not. But I got a job for you anyhow. The old Reynold's place up on Flat Ridge. There ain't no chance being caught. Even by God if that's a-worryin' you. It's all by its little lonesome up there, just beggin' for a visit by *the expert*. Nobody's lived there forever and the owners stand to make a pretty payday off the insurance. You do this job and we both make money, plus them."

Ed drew a long steadying breath. The tug of the fire was still there, like the old coal mines burning hundreds of feet underground. Never out. Always there in a slow, hot burn, quiet and dangerous.

"You healed up from that last job, are ya?"

"Barely. But like I said, I'm not interested." The healing blisters down his back tightened with chills.

Dillon stepped closer, studying down on Ed. The floor gave with Dillon's weight.

"Eddy, you and me go back. We got a lot of history tangled up between us. So much so, the way I see it, if I say you have a job to do, you'll just do it."

The voice raised in Ed's ear.

Save this man and we're even.

"I ain't droppin' this, Ed."

"I know you ain't."

Ed locked the front doors from outside, swiping his shirtsleeve over some glass. The large panes across the whole storefront wanted another cleaning. He'd just detailed them last week, but the coal trucks kicked up so much dust it was impossible. He looked up satisfied at the sign overhead emblazoned in red and black stretching down the awning: CHURCH OF THE HOLY FIRE OF GOD.

He had such big plans. The place was large, an old Dollar Time store. Plenty of room for a "let's stroll through hell" festival as a Halloween alternative. A sizeable food pantry. Counseling offices. They'd have a bus. Revivals in the parking lot. A newsletter. A website. There was money for it all, especially with decent offerings.

Wednesday morning Dillon slid into the booth across from Ed's steak-and-eggs breakfast at the Waffle Stop. Ed's appetite withered.

"I seen you praying there," Dillon jabbed, sipping his coffee.

"Yep." Ed crammed his mouth with a chunk of steak he hoped would keep him busy chewing rather than talking.

"You didn't used to."

Ed forced a swallow.

"Pray before every meal now." He bit a roll in half.

"Yea. You didn't use to do a lot of things. But some things you did do."

Ed sipped a loud gulp of coffee and smacked his lips.

"Why keep up this act?"

Ed thought on that a moment.

"Dillon, let me ask you something you might find odd. You think a person can tip the scales back in favor of their salvation?"

Dillon huffed. Ed's sudden and strange religion was testing his patience.

"That's what I'm doing. And this ain't no act. I'm making up for what I've done, for what I've done for you."

"Shit, man. You never hurt no one. Anyway, why do you think you was so good at fire buggin'?"

Ed put himself back into his old way of thinking. It was a good question.

"I liked to stay in it till I couldn't stand it no more. Something about it felt natural to me."

"I was thinking more along the fact that you just like it. Still like it."

Dillon leaned closer.

"You're a sick, fire-lovin' low-life. No better than any of us. You remember that, *preacher*. And don't get any bright ideas of being better than me with that ready cash you've got."

Ed managed a turn-the-cheek smile. Meant it.

"In the end, there's something else I'd rather do for you, Dillon."

"Oh, what's that?"

"Save your soul. From hell."

Dillon about sprayed coffee across the table.

"I've been there. You don't want none of it."

"You'll do the job, son. Or else."

Ed was in no good mood when he prayed that night.

Lord, if I can save, or help save, Dillon Hamby, that low-life, slum-pimp excuse of your handiwork, surely you'd forgive my innumerable sins in the end, right? Lord, you sure scraped the barrel with him, didn't you?

Ed was up on Flat Ridge by Friday night, staring the Reynold's place down in the blackness, reminded of Jesus and Satan wrestling it out in the wilderness. There he was, alone in the woods, with no help to fight off his demons. Just like the Lord out in the desert for forty days and nights.

The structure loomed, lightly framed along its roof line and corners by the half-hearted moon. His arms hung heavy with two cans of gasoline. If he was going to do this last job it was going to be done right. No good road remained and he'd sloshed the sweet stink of fuel on his shoe's tripping up the hill to the property.

Why was he here?

He'd tried to sleep, but would rise and pace, obsessed with temptation cloaked in Dillon's voice. Finally a drive in the dark was all he could manage. Then he'd found himself at the Quik Pick #2 for some gas. Elma had been working. He'd hesitated, barely back in since he'd won, too distracted by his new work, but mostly trying to break his habits. She was one of them old habits. They'd never gone out, never spoken anywhere other than that store. Collateral damage, he guessed. He turned on his heels and paid for the gas at the pump with his new debit card. He'd never even offered to pay her a tip for selling him that winning ticket. What an ass.

He'd driven, knowing he was bound right for where Dillon said he ought to be. Like a good errand boy, thoroughly cowed. It wasn't *what* a man like Dillon did that made him feared, it was what such a man *might do*. Imaginations grandly inflated his reputation, but not by much. Ed knew where all the bodies were, so to speak. Tempting Dillon over this house would surely run the risk of something bad eventually.

Now it was just him and his smoking ghosts, a hair from backsliding into the fire, to burn with the likes of Dillon.

But he wasn't alone.

You want to burn something?

The constant chatter confused him.

Burn your own place. This place is no business of yours.

Who was whispering so close up on his ear?

"Why would you say such a thing, God?"

Silence followed him off the hill.

Ed was on a roll Sunday morning. The pews were crowded and he had a belly full of frustration and praise to cast on the heads of his congregation. He felt like he'd binged on two pots of coffee, his skin crawling with goosebumps, heart thumping in his ears, throat strained, sweaty chills running his spine up to the back of his short-cropped head of hair, brain twisted up like a spring, sharp and ready. He felt drenched in the spirit.

The paint was only just dry on the baptistery he'd fashioned together all night. He patted the railing, proud of how it turned out, over four feet high and ten feet across. A small pool of sorts, trimmed in stained wood, full up with cool tap water he'd hosed from the kitchenette all morning long. By God, he'd baptize sinners in it today or die trying.

"God uses fire!" Ed yelled.

"All through the Bible. 'For the Lord thy God is a consuming fire, even a jealous God,' Deuteronomy 4:24. God speaks through the fire, punishes and destroys through the fire, warms us and heals us through fire! He doesn't speak much through the cold or ice, or through water. It's fire! I looked up the number of times fire and flame is mentioned in the King James Bible. Care to guess? Anybody?"

"A hundred," someone shouted.

"Nope."

"Three hundred?" another asked.

"Nope. Five hundred and fifty-one times! And this here baptistery—what getting baptized does for you—is replace that very real threat of hell-fire with the fire of the Holy Spirit!"

Dillon made his way in. He hadn't slept all night. His curiosity about Ed drove him to task. If he had to beat Ed to death in his own church he'd do it, but he would wait for the service to end before showing Ed the consequences of his stubbornness.

But what greeted Dillon when he settled truly took his breath. He was shocked. The back wall, behind Ed's pulpit, was stacked thick with white candles, over a hundred of them at least, lit and bouncing light all over the walls. Ed was hopping around on the stage screaming chapter and verse, shadowed and flickering with the jumpy candlelight. Something in Dillon's stomach dropped. He'd never seen such a sight.

"The burning bush! Fire pillars in the desert! Fire raining down on cities! The Day of Pentecost! Burnt offerings! Over and over! Now I don't want you all," Ed continued, staring through the dimness at who he made out to be Dillon, "bustin' hell wide-open. I want you all in Heaven with me. Ever, single, one of you."

Ed slipped a hand down as he shouted and snatched up a small glassless hurricane lamp. He fingered into his pocket and brought out his trusty Zippo, snapped it open, and lit it with three fingers, set the lamp wick aflame, and turned the knob full on. His face and chest glowed bright. He set the lamp down and rolled up his sleeves and raised his hands to the ceiling and closed his eyes in a quiet prayer. His arms were wrinkled in scars, shiny in the light, rippled past the elbows, evidence of his close waltz with the devil those strange months back.

He stalked the middle aisle, eye to eye with his people, now passing the lamp flame under his hand and wrist, a wisp of blackened smoke twisting from his fingertips. At first he looked like a magician, but the quick scent of smoked hair and flesh wafted out and someone gagged.

Ed's lit teeth gritted and dammed back the wellspring of pain, words hissing through a clenched jaw. He skipped back and leaned down face-to-face with Dillon. "By God's grace," he grimaced, "I know fire, brother." He winced and shook, lifting and dividing the flame in half up his along his forearm, a severe red blotch starting to char. "Believe me!"

Dillon's eyes stretched wide and he recoiled. The stench of it filled his nose, tightening his throat. The congregation was quiet but for their gasps of disbelief.

"This here's nothing compared to the soul-consuming destiny waiting on the unsaved! The damned! The devil's own children!"

Someone whispered their wonder as to how Ed stood such pain.

Ed jerked the flame away finally, teetering on the precipice of blacking out. The people sighed relief in unison. Dillon was frozen in amazement.

"You don't think I felt every second of that, people?" he winced. "Yes! Yes, I did." He saw stars down the aisle back to the pulpit. Back to the baptistry. "But that's nothing compared to where I might have gone had the Lord not intervened in my sorry life!"

He hadn't broken eye contact with Dillon, who was squirming and nauseous now.

Ed spoke low, "And you don't think I'm willing to do anything necessary on behalf of God's Kingdom? Be it pain or suffering? God's will be done."

The pain numbed and the energy surged back and Ed sprinted down the aisle and did a one-handed hop into the baptistery, splashing feet first, dipping his arm into the coolness of the water, sucking in a long breath and smiled with obvious joy.

"Who among you will be baptized this day?!"

"I will," someone shouted, bolting into the aisle. Then another came.

Eight baptisms in, Ed turned to help another step down into the water and met a face he did not expect. Dillon. The candles illuminated a kind of smile he'd never seen on Dillon's face, the evidence of tears filling the corners of his eyes. Some kind of epiphany working through the man's brain.

Lord, Almighty, sprang to Ed's thoughts, *what have you blessed or cursed me with here?*

He helped Dillon down into the waist-deep waters and raised his right hand, supporting Dillon's back with the left.

There were murmurs in the congregation. Perhaps of disbelief. Partly that Ed would be baptizing anyone for anything. Partly that Dillon was in baptismal waters. That any of this was anything more than a joke. God had to be in this for it to be happening.

"As Jesus taught, those who confess me before men and are baptized will live forever."

He pulled up close to Dillon, staring into his eyes and talking too low for anyone to hear.

"You for real?"

Dillon nodded.

Don't believe him.

"I'm suspicious."

The organ played over their conversation.

"We don't believe you, you son of a bitch," Ed hissed, leaning Dillon back. "We baptize thee in the name of the Father . . ."

"We who?" Dillon questioned as his full body fell back into the water.

He came here to hurt you.

Ed popped Dillon back up.

" . . . the Son . . ." Down again, back up and down.

Dillon's nose and mouth filled with the sweet sting of gasoline as he rose for the third time.

If he's not telling the truth this man will kill you.

" . . . and the Holy Ghost . . ."

Dillon's eyes stung shut. He tried to right himself, confused, heavy wet, coughing and flailing as the sting set into his skin and face. He squinted harder to see.

Ed was splashing gasoline from a milk jug over him, soaking his clothes. Soaking both of them down to the skin.

Violent fingers clamped around Dillon's large arm, tugging with authority, a heavy menace in Ed's breathing. Whatever was on him was on Ed, too, soaking them, rain-bowing across the rippling surface of the baptismal water, fumes saturating the air around them.

Someone on the front row gasp. Sounded like they were scrambling away.

The distinct snap and clink of a lighter halted dead still any struggle from Dillon.

Dillon recognized that lighter through his squinting, the chrome flash, the faded flames. How deftly Ed could flick it even during the struggle.

"Shall we test our faith, brother Dillon?"

Day of the Dead Diner, Home of Juan D's Best BBQ

665 1/2 Eller Creek Lane is just off Highway 33. The one building on the property looks like a typical joint: a plain front, gravel lot, a generic sign board running the top where anything might get painted or latched across once something moved in. Bannisters along a sort of long porch on the front. It's got metal double doors in the middle with no glass. Not a terribly inviting place.

The community complained for years when it was known as the Dusk Drifter Lounge, or the DDL (AKA a hangout for the Dead, Damned, and Lame). As fine a place as any to get stabbed or shot if you were in the mind for it. Consistently blind drunk for sure. Regulars loved it like regulars would. Most just tolerated the regular arrival of ambulances and rumors of who got hurt on past weekends and who was throwing down the gauntlet to get it on for the coming weekend.

The owner, Jo Ray, never claimed any fault, of course. Cruddy people were idiots and he only provided the alcoholic lube to bring out the legitimate dumbasses festering inside everyone, he'd boast. Cheap beer, tequila, and long about sometime after 11 p.m.

on a Saturday night was when his lubing philosophy did its best business.

But along the mid-eighties, Jo got bad sick and things went even more to hell if you can believe that. Patrons were shot, and broken, and stuck before, but never ended up so bad off they were dead. Eventually a guy was beaten to death out back and left at the bottom of the grease trap for a week. Jo got sued over it, but they never got a dime out of him. He had a massive stroke before he was indicted for negligence. Everyone knew he'd lose. Hell, the man was so sorry even the batteries on his fake security cameras were dead.

They found him facedown on his own bar early one Monday morning. They guessed he'd been there since closing up from Saturday's shift. He was death number two after the boy in the grease box.

His older sister Diana and younger sister Sheila Sue, both of which worked at the DDL for years, fought over the place in probate court for over a year. They ended up selling it down the middle and walking off in a huff swearing never to look at the other again, let alone talk. They arranged to attend the funeral home and graveside service for their brother in separate shifts.

Sam Greene bought the place next, replaced the old grease trap, and opened Sam's Taco Heaven. His mistake was keeping the old bar open and trying for a Mexican feel with "Margarita Mondays." Someone else was dead a little over a year later, run over in the parking lot when an unsanctioned Cinco de Mayo MMA fight was busted by the state boys. Everyone scattered when the authorities arrived and hit the lights and sirens and a girl got run over in the parking lot.

It sat empty for a couple of years, layered in strange graffiti inside and out and was about to get condemned as a meth den until two Labor County magistrates had the bright idea to turn it into a golf lunch club. As far as they were concerned, the sun rose and sat in the ass crack of the ancient and honorable game of golf, so they started moving dirt out back to open a three-hundred-yard driving range.

One of them, Peter Buskins, a contractor, loved playing in the dirt. Well, he should have left that to his workers. He was out there by himself messing with his toy equipment, pushing trees down, and one popped back on the cab of the dozer and pinned him most of Sunday and into Monday morning before one of his underpaid employees found him. Everyone said he should have been in church on Sunday instead of out tearing up God's green earth.

By then everyone pretty much agreed the place was cursed.

Yet people kept sinking stupid money into it.

A husband and wife opened it up as a hotdog and ice cream shop—the Cool Doggy Dog's Doghouse—but it caught fire, killed Emily the wife, and made the husband, David, rich from the insurance pay out. Everyone suspected arson, but who was going to really investigate the intentional burning of a hotdog hut? Where David went off to after that, no one knew, but people assumed he had sand between his toes wherever it was.

Some high schoolers had the brilliant idea to set the place up as a Halloween haunted house during the business failings. It ended up being a great spot for the Labor County Red Devils Haunted House and Annual Full-Service Car Wash fundraisers. The football cheerleaders, dressed as zombies, would wash your car while the football team and booster families inside the building tried scaring the shit out of you. It was a good time for everyone and no one ever died, which was a surprise.

The Day of the Dead Diner was the brainchild of Juan Diablo-Mullins, originally out of Wretcher County. When Juan's mother, Sandra, was finished with the place, with all the bright yellow and orange and green and red, and all the colorful skulls no one really understands these days, but love to slap on T-shirts all the time, it was a destination reborn. Plus, Sandra reputedly made the best homemade tamales in five states. She rolled them in corn shucks especially brought up from Mexico.

By the time Juan was opening the restaurant, people were losing track of how many deaths had occurred there on the property. That was fine by Juan. He and his family would change the reputation of the place. What people didn't know wouldn't hurt them.

The next unfortunate soul was a drifter who wandered off Highway 33 one afternoon. A shady looking guy, begging a job from "Juan D"—as some knew him—as he cleaned up the place readying the upcoming weekend grand opening festivities.

Juan D was feeling gracious, so he let the new guy help clean out the walk-in freezer. They talked. The man was only walking through town. From somewhere up north. Headed south. No one knew him. He was a hard worker and Juan D appreciated help.

The guy never left the walk-in freezer that afternoon. By the end of the day that guy was in easily wrapped bits, neatly stacked for future use. Unrecognizable as anything but meat in that very freezer they'd both organized during the day.

The blood was a sacrifice of thanksgiving. Juan D's heart was glad to have the ceremony out of the way so quickly and unexpectedly.

He sighed to himself cleaning up the mess. *Thank Santa Ella of new endeavors.*

His heart was thrilled by the signs-smeared tiled floor of the kitchen, the grounds now sanctified and satisfied for at least a year. He glanced up at a burning candle effigy of a red-robed female over the stainless-steel stove. Her skulled face already melted down to the shoulders, long red drips making way down her robe, over her skeletal hands. There would be none of these unexpected deaths like the other owners had suffered over the years. The kind of incidents leading to tragedies. Business failures. Heartbreak. If anyone died from here on out, it would be planned and useful. Blood witnessed by the ancient patron saint of sustenance. Blood sacrifice.

We thank Santa Ella for these many blessings and those to come.

Juan D invited a few friends over for one hell of a celebratory BBQ that evening. He'd worked the meat all day with his new split-hinged fifty-five-gallon drum smoker. That beauty of a cooker would be lifeblood of the Diablo-Mullins family business. The center-piece of their soon-to-be-famous annual nonviolent BBQ blowouts. Free for the whole community.

Brotherhood of the Mystic Hand

The call might come anytime during the first half of May, the traditional salutation: "Who's got the hand?"

According to established bylaws, whoever drew the short straw at the last gathering, minus that year's host, would be officially invested with possession of "The Hand" and be granted the esteemed responsibility of making preparations for the coming year's reunion. Now that might be where the organizer lived (usually boring), or any other obscure location they could dream up (preferred). That was the game, to guarantee the Annual Headhunters Reunion of grizzled grunts was as memorable as they could stomach.

The traditional reply to "Who's got the hand," say, if Jeffrey Adams up in Acres, Kentucky, had it one year, was: "That fuck'n short-timer Jeffrey's got the hand. Lucky son of a bitch!" After that you could proceed with the normal conversation between old buddies about the upcoming Vietnam reunion and whatever crazy spot Jeffrey was dreaming up where everyone was obligated to travel. Rules were important. Rules are necessary. It's what got everybody back from the jungle. Knowing the rules and knowing when to break them.

When Earl Johnson of Labortown called up his best buddy Loren Mason over in Harlan and inquired as per usual, "Who's got the hand?" it was unfortunate Earl hadn't heard the news. He'd take it hard. Loren hesitated at first, which he wasn't apt to do being an old comms man. He usually knew exactly what to say in every situation.

"Well . . . that fuck'n short-timer . . . Randy . . . used to, Loren. But the son of a bitch bought it last week, buddy. Stroke."

Earl fell quiet. This was highly out of the ordinary.

"Sarg, this is highly out of the ordinary."

"I know, man. His wife, Frieda, just called me this morning."

"This is terrible," Earl whispered, more to himself than to his buddy.

"She's a damn wreck."

Another long pause.

"But he had the hand," Earl reminded Loren.

"I know. I know. Frieda said he'd just managed all the arrangements for the meet somewhere outside Wilmington, North Carolina, so we're good. Some little dive bar out near a beach. Word's going around about him dyin' and all."

"What about him? I mean . . ."

"Reckon we're gonna be having our first funeral-slash-reunion. We've had men die off, but never when they've had *the hand* in possession. You might want to add something to the by-laws about this when everything's died down."

"No pun intended," Earl joked.

"Yep. I meant that one."

"Oh."

"So who's got the hand? I mean now?"

"Frieda's delivering the hand. Don't you worry about that none. Along with his ashes."

"Jesus. This is gonna be a strange one. More than usual."

Earl heard Loren tearing down through Dry Hollow long before any dust cloud the old 47 Harley Knucklehead sidecar combo could manage coughing up over the pines. It was loud as hell. He could feel it in his feet through the planks of the house.

"You can't sneak up on anybody," Earl complained once Loren killed the famous V-twin engine's grumble.

"Don't got to any more do we, killer?"

"True. We can wake hell all the way for all I care."

"It's a far piece to get there, that's for sure."

Earl set in to his usual routine, strapping what little gear he had to the sidecar with bungie cords, half of the weight surely bourbon and strong beer Loren figured, weight that would become lighter as the miles ticked off into the night. Loren could tell he'd already been at it by the sweet hovering smell round the porch.

"You have any breakfast?" Loren asked.

"If liquid bread counts, yep."

They'd head down through the Smoky Mountains and ride Highway 40 all the way through North Carolina to the coast at Wilmington, where the road quit at the sea, and then search out their final destination. It was Thursday evening. They had two days.

A bungie snapped loose and popped Earl on the back of the hand, causing a salvo of old Vietnamese curse phrases out of Earl's repertoire of useless language learnings.

"You need any help there, killer?" Loren offered, watching his buddy struggle with the gear. Earl turned, shooting his well-known aggravated pop-eyed look. He pointed at Loren with what served as his left hand, two finely sharpened stainless-steel hooks.

"I'll ask for what I need when I need it, old man."

Loren just laughed.

"You'll walk, too. I'll just tell everybody you fell out along the way and I never noticed."

"You thirsty."

"Somebody's got to drive this she-monster, don't I?"

"True," Earl admitted, hiking a leg up and the other into the sidecar and settling in, and plopping his black shiny helmet on. "Let's get there in one piece." He saluted with the hooks and offered a buzzed grin.

"Always do."

These two traveled together every year, ever since Loren acquired the sidecar Harley seven years ago. He bragged that the special paint job alone was as expensive as getting the wreck roadworthy after finding it junked out in a parts lot in LA. The paint was black and gold, the traditional First Cav colors, the division the Headhunters Troop was attached to during the war. It was hard to miss such a work of art hauling ass down the highway, loud and proud both in bright and bold colors and rumbling sound, turning heads. Their old unit patch was on the broadness of the sidecar, a round patch with a simple white, empty-eyed skull with yellow flames licking up from the scalp. A spear rammed through both temples and the word *Headhunters* curled underneath in red. The message was pretty clear for anyone with any sense of well-being. *Been there, done that, move along.*

Knowing another twenty-seven fellow be-dragglers were crawling way across the land to this year's chosen location gave the air a special kind of zing. This Headhunter's Reunion was number seventeen. They remained a motley collection of special-ops warriors scattered to the winds and such a reunion was the only way to come together. They still needed each other. After what they'd been through, after what they'd seen each other through, what the country had put them through, *their country*, they needed to see each other through to the end. The very end.

And now another was gone.

Imagine you're nineteen in Southeast Asia. Imagine being free of a wife or girlfriend, any connections to speak of, really. Socking away most of your money. Banking combat pay on top of that. You're sniper-trained. Expert in jungle survival, escape, and evasion. Interrogation. Grab-and-go operations. Assassinations. Working out in the bush for months, until your fatigues were rotting off. Then maybe half a month of hardcore R&R. Working in headhunting teams of seven. If you can stay alive in all this, the world is your oyster, right? You're a badass, Uncle Sam trained to the molecular level. A *you-don't-die-until-you-get-his-permission-in-writing* sort of thing. Assassin gods of the jungle complex, etc.

Earl loved it with all his heart. He'd reupped and was on his third tour in sixty-nine already. And he didn't take it all for granted. He respected every day above the bug crawling jungle ground he got. Every life of the enemy he cut short. Unfortunately, as he liked to colorfully explain to curious millennials who weren't even damp spots in their Gen X daddy's drawers yet, "I zigged when I ought to have zagged one night in the fine Republic of Vietnam, and a Commie's point five-one caliber round shot most of my left hand off above the wrist." He'd point where a huge round would have hit and left his hand hanging.

After they'd *ooh* and *ah*, he'd continue to explain that the war was not going to wait for him to deal with a dangling hand so he just had the medic slice the rest off since it was mostly skin attached. He'd wrapped it up in a captured VC flag he kept on him. He snuck out while in the hospital and had some papa-san preserve the thing before it went too rotten and shipped it home to his mother, Mary. She'd never forgiven him for not warning her what was in the package box. She must have opened it up expecting the usual pretties "from the orient." It was pretty alright. She about fainted.

Earl was a short man. Barely the height necessary to get in the service. But what he lacked in stature in his young years was put in balance by sheer ignorant meanness when he needed it in the field. His buddies said he was too crazy to die. "They don't let people like you in heaven or hell," they'd tell him. When they nicknamed him "Killer," they'd meant it.

A little old age down in the back now shortened him by another inch or two and a drink or three or four relaxed him another inch, so on a good day he was barely over five feet. That, along with the hooks and the hand mythology, made him the group's human mascot, which was a character he enjoyed playing. If anything, it was just their way of keeping him and his friendly Napoleon complex out of jail every meeting. He got antsy when he left Kentucky. Said flat land made him nervous. These get-togethers were about the only time he left his home county now.

Their 501-c-3 status for fundraising may have informed the nosey government they were the Headhunters Club, but to Earl and the rest, they were the "Brotherhood of the Mystic Hand," purchased with true sweat, tears, and good old American flesh, blood, and bone at the expense of a well-gut-splattered Southeast Asian jungle.

If Loren ever inherited a tendency for alcoholism he'd have given in years ago listening to Earl tell this story. Death by a thousand tellings, Loren nicknamed it. And here they were, long past midnight in some dive outside Raleigh, road weary but still thirsty and Earl catching a second wind after already passing out on the road and coming to. He had these two birds at the bar wrapped around one of the fingers of his remaining hand, so to speak.

Earl's secret weapon wasn't what he had, but what he was missing. That hand. That damn hand. And he had these girls, who had a sexy allotment of tattoos and piercings, seen and unseen, all worked up about what and where he could continue any piercings they needed with his hand-o'-hooks. They were about ready to leave with him—headed God-knows-where—until he spilled the beans he was riding shotgun on a sidecar. After that they'd excused themselves to the ladies' room.

"Think they went to get some friends?" Loren ribbed him.

"Screw you, two-hander."

"Get in and we'll head down to the rest stop. Get some shut eye," Loren suggested, feeling bad for Earl standing outside the bar speculating on which way the girls had fled.

"You jinxed me, man. You're always doin' that," he mumbled through the haze he seemed to keep stoked no matter where the sun was shining.

"I never said a word."

"That don't matter none. You was there."

"Let's go, killer."

They slept in their surplus olive, drab 'Nam-era sleeping bags under a North Carolina pine with low-hanging branches for a few hours, but their snoring would have given away their position had anyone cared to be looking for them. They'd learned long ago that most people this time of night at rest stops left others alone for good reason.

Those sleeping bags they were in, complete with a color that seemed to couldn't wear out of the heavy cotton and canvass after these decades, were typical accoutrements of this group of men. They refused normal camping bags, preferring that old Vietnam era army green. This drab-green aesthetic permeated the men's lives. Hanging on to old tools of the trade, things they despised once, associated with death and pain, but chose to claim now, bound by that color of the deadened jungle mood, bonded them as brothers in a way only a glance required. That's all it took to tell another what he was about and what he'd probably been through since the late sixties.

Cicadas cranked up their whining drones before seven. Earl rolled over, wanting to yell at them for being so loud and hurting his head. It was already getting warm and traffic heading into and out of Raleigh was getting heavy. Loren was on the phone with Frieda.

"Amos is down near Belleville. He'll wait. Frieda's already at the beach and getting things settled. Others are getting there."

"You tell her I said hey?"

Loren huffed. "No, man, I didn't." He cocked a brow. "You planning on making an ass of yourself down here?"

Earl didn't answer that. "C'mon. Let's go see the Mustache Man."

Amos was an odd one. Odd even among this odd lot. A lifelong bachelor, he never stayed anywhere very long, fancying himself a professional bohemian. A renegade poet, some said, though even he knew not what he was renegade from, so at least he had a sense of humor about his reputation.

A blackish-green 1969 Lincoln Continental Mark III was parked like a long dark boat in front of a pure white Catholic church. It was an ominous scene, missing only a fog machine's ambiance. It was the seven-foot retired medical-school instructional skeleton Amos kept in the back seat that fully set the mood, however. A back window was down. The skeleton wore a vintage ladies' felt hat with face netting pulled down over an eye socket. A ratty mink pelt wrapped its skinny neck vertebrae. Two strings of fat faux pearls. A Mardi Gras necklace. A stuffed leather brassier and matching miniskirt with knee-high red Patton leather stiletto boots. This was Amos's constant companion, the "Widow Jenny."

Amos sported a wide handlebar mustache that took him, he claimed, no less than an hour of coifing each morning, an immaculately clean-shaven chin and jaw, Ray-Bans, and a thick braid of red hair down the center of his head and down half his back and tied off with a rough strip of what he claimed was black-stained North Carolina opossum leather.

"Who's got your hand, Earl?" Amos jabbed with a joking smile as Loren and Earl pulled up and killed the rumble of the Harley.

Earl smirked. "Frieda."

"Yeah. Shame about Randy and all. But we all gotta go some-time, right Jennifer?" Amos commented back to the skeleton. "Still, we're gonna tie one on anyways, right?"

"Been doin' that for a couple hundred miles now," Loren offered, more about his passenger than himself, though he was getting jeal-ous about now.

Earl just grinned, half-asleep. "How you doin', Jenny?" He about expected her to answer back they were so used to her by now. "Nice new mink, by the way."

"You want point?" Amos offered up.

"Only if you're good with staying at about sixty-five. That's about all I can do with this dead weight here." He nodded at Earl.

"Let him sleep in the back seat to the coast and let's see if we can keep it at seventy or more?"

"Deal. I was tired of smellin' him, even at sixty-five. All he does is sweat alcohol. A man gets jealous after a while."

"Screw you, ten fingers," Earl muttered stumbling into the back of the Continental. "Scooch, Jenny." He was probably asleep before he got comfortable across the slick original black leather, his head on his own pillow he'd been sitting on in the sidecar, now softly re-laxing in the "Widow's" boney but welcomed lap.

"Hellfire, son! You look like a piece of pig grizzle that's been cookin' on the nasty hood of my truck."

"Yea, well you'd still eat half my ass if you were hungry, wouldn't you?"

As soon as Loren and Earl and Amos walked into Tank's Tavern in Carolina Beach, North Carolina, the burly man insulting Loren so intimately was bear-hugging all of them. Loren didn't even have a comeback out yet. Then just as quickly there were raised beer bottles and mugs sloshed in the air and a loud group *hurrah* and a year's worth of catching up to get started on.

"I see brunch is still available," Earl happily commented with a smile as he hopped up on a bar stool and slapped the backs of the men on each side of him. "I need a drink. My back's stiff and my neck's crooked. I feel like I've been asleep in the arms of death in the back of a car all mornin' or somethin'."

Someone was already handing him a mug of beer to get him started.

"And by the way. Where's my damn hand?"

Wherever they landed each year, it quickly felt as if they were all relaxing at some home hangout, and whatever business hosted them usually played along. Randy's pick was perfect.

Tank's Tavern, established 1979, might have been an iffy hole in the wall joint, but it wasn't always so small a spot. Tank Jackson, proprietor, had sacrificed bar space for, "Carlene II," the M113 Armored Personnel Carrier, or APC, taking up the footprint of at least three parking spaces or additional drinking room. It was named after the pretty girl he was seeing when he shipped off for the "police action" in Korea in 1950. Unfortunately that girl who'd promised to wait for him ended up with someone else's last name by the time he'd survived the Battle of the Chosin Reservoir, minus a frozen foot he'd left in a trench.

Tank was kind of shell-shocked along with missing the right foot and nursing a head tremor. For a man owning a "tavern" and a cabin boat where he resided most of the year, this was a natural invitation for him to have fashioned a well-fitting wooden prosthetic peg leg which rounded out his year-round pirate persona. He'd brass-capped the tip for a nice *thunk*. The wood floor was destroyed with scratches and dents, evidence of Tank's peg leg from over the years.

Luckily one of the advantages of having the APC was its serving as eye candy for vets and the fact that many of them had spent what felt like lifetimes in these "iron coffins." Most of them didn't mind the heat then, so it basically became the outdoor smoking room where you could drink. Tank belched the loud diesel engine up only once a year—Memorial Day—not even on Veterans Day—though there was a story of some regulars trying to steal the keys and take it for a ride on several occasions. That's why Tank claimed to have the carburetor hidden somewhere off the property.

Frieda reported that with stories like this on Tank's website, Randy was real proud of the place he'd found for this year's get-together. He was looking forward to gloating over having found the coolest spot ever.

Earl heard Frieda's voice over all the bar's noise, her sweet Georgia drawl easily lilting above the crowd, seeking wounded ears. Randy had fallen for that, her voice, and the rest of her, the very first night they'd met, the night Earl introduced them fifteen years ago. She was working the bar Earl liked to drink at down in Chatsworth. *The Heartbreaker*. He figured Randy might like her. But when they hit it off that well, Earl hadn't ever quite been the same about it. He'd go hug her and say he was sorry after he got another drink sloshing in his belly.

As crowded as the place was, the guys still managed to sort of line up down the crowded bar, behind those seated at the stools, to offer condolences to Frieda. She was down at the end of the L-shaped bar, on the last stool around the corner, sipping on a gin and tonic no one ever let run low. Positioned in front of her and beside her drink was a tall antique blue mason jar full of grayish-white chalky powder that had to be what was left of good old Randy. Looks like

Randy had napalm for lunch, Earl thought to himself. At least he was here, sitting on the bar with all the guys, with his wife. Someone had a tequila shot poured and sitting beside the jar along with a scribbled sign reading, *Fuck you, Randy!*

And, of course, balanced on top of the jar was the only thing in the room odd enough to cause more of a stir than a body's cremated remains, Earl's mummified left hand in all its pedestaled and dried-out creepy glory. Occasionally, one of the men would grab it by the steel-shank base that was rammed into the wrist and lift it high, demanding everyone's attention for a toast, announcing: "He who lifts the Mystic Hand, your attention does demand!" Word was Amos had come up with that little dandy.

Earl would get in line eventually. He just wasn't ready. What would he say? He couldn't tell if he wanted to be drunker or soberer to talk to Frieda.

The bar was a din of toasts and hollers and tears and hugs and kisses and fists on the bar and swears of brotherhood and reminiscences and smoky, beer breathings, and calls for new rounds. And this was only Friday evening. Hell, everyone hadn't even arrived yet and a few were already about to pass out.

They'd rolled in from places stretching from Alaska to Florida. One from Canada. Alfred Lemarr was living along the Mexican–American border now, Mexico side. And since Randy had bit the dust, attendance was higher than usual.

The bar was bookended by an out-of-business, sterilized-looking realty office on one side along with the tiny parking lot crowded with the squared-off dark-green armored vehicle. With all the congregating sixty-somethings laughing in bursts, smoking their cigarettes or stogies, a few sneaking around the corner for a little weed, seeming afraid of nothing, chummed up, dressed in olive-green, drab jackets, the distinctive black caps of today's 'Nam era vets, it was obvious at a glance that something big was going on. Add to that scene the bikes and cars of particular character and the message might as well have been in temporary neon out front, flashing up the street: seventy-two-hour party in progress. Regulars displaced. Join at own risk.

Tank was happy. The regulars weren't. The place hadn't been that crowded since the Motley Crew tribute band—Motley Dudes—played for free at the pavilion across the street last summer.

When Earl caught Tank eyeing his hooked hand with a covetous look, he gave Tank his best pop-eyed stare. "I come from a long line of pirate hunters you ol' coot. Stop eyein' my hooks and earn your own the hard way." Tank guffawed at that and bought him another.

Earl and Tank got along pretty good since both of them were missing parts. "I wasn't sure what to make of that Frieda woman setting up that hand at first," Tank admitted. "Thought maybe she was point woman for some cult I hadn't vetted good enough."

"That hand's survived many a close call," Earl explained. Getting out of the jungle was the simplest trick, apparently. Earl told Tank how an ex-girlfriend had accidently, on purpose, sold the thing at a yard sale once and how Loren and him had spent a week running it back down and it costing him three hundred dollars when the man had bought if for ten at the sale. How Jimmy had almost incinerated it once when he'd lined a bar in St. Louis with Maker's Mark and lit it without grabbing the hand up. And especially how many dogs had been caught in the act of burying it.

Local ordinances required Tank to close up the front doors by three in the morning, but since he kept an efficiency apartment upstairs, the party sort of moved in and out of that space and onto the tiny patio out back and quietly to the APC for a hardcore few. Old Man Time eventually hunts down the meanest old warriors and half the crew wandered off for some shut eye eventually, sensing they'd have to pace themselves or end up wasting time sleeping off hangovers in good daylight. A handful got shut up in the bar sleeping. Another few just slept it off in the APC or up in the apartment and didn't bother finding their ways to hotels they never managed checking in to anyway. Someone said they found Earl down on the beach sleeping up in a lifeguard tower with his shirt off and his flip-flops rolling in the surf. That Amos slept in his car with the "Widow Jenny" wasn't out of the ordinary.

Things were fine until Saturday afternoon when Earl heard someone giggling something low-voiced about *Captain Hook over here*. He just couldn't manage to take Loren's advice and take a breath and *let it go, let it go*, like that cartoon song suggested. He was sensitive about the hooks after all.

"I'm sorry, fellas," he broke in, turning all friendly like, loud enough for his own friends to hear. "Did you have a question about my hand?" He had the hooks up in the closest one's face so they could see it clearly. They weren't kids, probably twenty-somethings. The one that seemed like he wanted to play this scenario out had his baseball cap on side-crooked with a bill he'd refused to break. His sunglasses were on backward, too, on the back of his head. The guy's girl was hugged up beside him, cautious now.

"We were wondering, yes. . . . um . . . how you, well . . . wipe your ass with that thing?" He cackled loud at his own joke, but realized quickly enough he was the only one laughing.

Earl smiled and furled his brow, as if he'd not thought on that predicament for a while. "Oh, I get along pretty good, being an old disabled war vet and all," he replied, playing along. "Miss, could I get another beer, please!"

"Here let me show y'all."

The girl leaned in. As deftly as a regularly handed man might, Earl demonstrated, holding the beer with his right, snapping the can tab with a hook, then reaching over to angle the adjustments on the hooks just right with a pull and a twist, he shoved the can in with enough denting to keep it snug in the hooks, at which point he commenced to up turn it and chug it down with only three swallows.

With that the smartass was both impressed and confused.

"Well hell, why didn't you just turn it up with your empty right hand. That's kinda stupid, don't you think?"

Some of the men were already stepping back.

"Not really," Earl replied, looking at the empty beer in his left hooks, distracting the kid. "I'm right-handed." By that time Earl had drawn back with his unoccupied fist and struck the guy across the jaw just enough to stun him good before everyone was fast enough to separate them. The kid admitted afterward he'd had it coming.

Everyone was stumbling down to the beach by midnight. Loren and a few others had already gathered up enough rocks for a pit during the day and the bonfire was blazing up taller than everyone's heads by now, spare wood appearing out of nowhere and no one was asking as long as some boat in the marina didn't get reported as sinking the next morning.

Wind from a storm moving in would push in and kick the flames sideways, tumbling red ash devils down the sand, casting odd flickering light across everyone's face as they wandered up and claimed a spot around the fire. A somberness was finally setting in as the weekend was wrapping up. The alcohol was taking its physical toll. The loss of Randy, its reminder of everyone's mortality, working mentally on everyone.

Earl was down along the water's edge. Frieda noticed and walked down. It was strange seeing him there, shin deep in the foaming surf, his own mummified hand clutched in his hooks. The shriveled thing was looking more worse than usual for the wear. She watched him trace one of his dead left-handed fingers with the tip of a living one. How strange that must be, even after all these damned years.

"Hey, Early." She was about the only one that could get away with calling him that.

He jumped a little. "Oh. Hey, girl. You spooked me."

"You ain't hardly said boo to me all weekend, hun."

"Yea, I guess so. I'm sorry."

She tried to change the subject.

"That thing freaked me out a bit haulin' it here in the car. Had to put it in the trunk finally. Felt like it wanted to crawl out of the box while I wasn't lookin'."

He gave it another look. "Shoot. This ain't my hand no more. Ain't been for a long time."

"What are you talkin' about?" she questioned, noticing just how drunk he was.

"A lot of stuff ain't me anymore." He gave a huff, fighting to stand straight in the surf. "Drinkin's killin' me, Frieda. Has been." He gave a long, tired huff.

"We all know that. That why you've been at it so much harder this weekend?"

He nodded. "Out with a bang. If I have to quit, I'm gonna remember the last hangover."

She wondered if he was sincere. This time.

"You gonna have help for it?"

"The hangover?"

"You know what I mean, silly."

"I'll manage." He paused, giving the darkness out over the water a longer look. A quick streak of silent lightning way out there brought him back.

"Jesus, I'm sorry about Randy, Frieda," he finally offered, barely audible over the sound of the waves coming in harder.

She didn't answer, staring at the same thing he was out there. Sighing. "It was just too fast. I wanted more time."

"It's awful."

"Well, don't get me started," she told him, wiping her eyes.

"And Frieda . . ."

She knew where this was going before he went there. Where it had to go now with Randy gone. Where the unspoken goes when the dam breaks. "Don't . . ." She wouldn't see Early again for a while, and he was drunk. He couldn't help himself.

"I'm sorry. I'm sorry I almost fucked it up for you all back then."

"Early. I said don't. It's water gone under the bridge, baby."

His words slurred. "Yea, but . . . it ain't never changed how I felt. You know that."

"Hush now."

"I always do just shut up about it. And I know I ought not be talking like this now, but . . ."

She was already walking away, stomping up the beach, back to the bonfire.

God. I'm an asshole.

He turned, dizzier, nauseous, a puking coming on. Feeling blind the surf was so black to his front. He had to piss and thought about letting it fly there over the waves, giggling to himself at the thought of one man polluting the whole ocean, but with the mummified hand in his hooks and his motor skills collapsing the way they were he thought better of it. He turned and shuffled back the best he could in the direction of the bonfire's flashing.

"To Randy!" someone toasted yet again in the firelight when Earl finally returned to the bonfire. Frieda was sitting on a stump by Loren. "To Randy!" she echoed, "My baby!" lifting her unsteady gin for the hundredth time. Others echoed her. Loren shot Earl a look like don't come too close, but Earl had other plans.

"To our brother!" rang out Earl's voice over everyone, obviously wanting to be heard. He spoke with both hands up. The Mystic Hand was held high, up in the hooks, a drink in Earl's fleshly hand.

"To a fine warrior." Men mumbled in agreement.

"To his good wife." He bowed to Frieda. She nodded, sleepy-eyed.

"To good men, all around!" More cheers. "To our brother, Randy." He sacrificed a small pour of his bourbon into the fire with a spitting hiss. A few others followed suit, causing the fire to fit up and rage.

"And now, brothers," Earl went on, "I have one final act on this special night, to commemorate our most unusual meeting of the Mystic Hand and the Headhunter's Club . . ."

He raised the hand higher. He glanced over, hoping for an instant of eye contact from Frieda. "Let us forgive each other our many trespasses."

Someone offered an *amen*. Earl looked at his good hand, then at the mummified hand clamped by the hooks.

"The time has come. It's time to retire it, brothers."

And with that, he doused bourbon all over his stuffed hand and dashed the relic down into the heart of the bonfire with the grand finale of a small impressive explosion.

Someone yelled out, "Hey! Hey! What the fuck, Earl?" Others cheered their crazy friend on, unsurprised. Earl just inhaled big and let out a big whooping yell. He could swear he saw the hand in the flames giving him the finger. *No. Fuck you*, he thought.

Earl, deathly ill, was trying to wake up a few hours later, but the road was calling them back home. He was nursing a hangover even he could hardly stand. He wanted a beer to settle his belly, but he was serious about quitting for good. It was time.

"You gonna regret tossing you're hand in the fire last night? You were pretty lit, even for you, man. You remember doin' it?"

Earl grinned, knowing he'd finally crossed a line. For good or ill, something had to give. He hoped he'd started some cleansing in the head, symbolically at least.

"Oh, I remember it. Plain as day, man. Or night, at least."

"I'm sure you knew what you're doing."

Earl knew Loren deserved the truth. Finally.

"Hell, Loren. I might as well come clean. With you of all people at least."

Loren wondered what he was about to find out.

"Listen, man. My hand was clean blowed all to pieces back in the bush. Shit. I couldn't even find a fingernail when it was all over. That thing last night? That we've been trottin' round for years? I cut that thing off a dyin' VC in the jungle and sent it to mom as a souvenir."

Loren shook his head, trying to believe what he was hearing.

"And you know what? I hope that feller lived after all. I pray to God he's been walkin' around all this time missing a hand just like me, knowing some crazy American sawed it off in a firefight in some worthless valley in some worthless war on some worthless day and spared his life, but sent his hand home as a souvenir for the rest of both of our shitty lives. And I hope last night he felt something give just a little. And slept a little better, finally."

Uncle Archie's Acquisition

I would have protected any secret in the world weird Uncle Archie required for that promised full skeleton of the last legally hanged man from Reilly County, Kentucky (and yes, I realized at a later age—an embarrassingly much later age—there never was such a thing as a Reilly County, Kentucky). All I had to do was keep my "damn teenage mouth" shut about the newly acquired cryotube I'd helped him drag into the back room of his continually wacked-out museum of a house.

His obsession increased with every year after retirement from the power company. Dad claimed all those years climbing around live wires had not only proven his machismo, but his strangeness upstairs in the brains department as well. Rewired him neurologically with that constant electromagnetic exposure. What was once a harmless hobby had turned into a hoarding of the god-awfullest strangeness you've ever seen. A strangeness I learned in time to love.

But he wasn't just blindly packing his house with dangerous piles of fire-prone junk, with uncontrolled slush piles where old pets went missing and turned up later, petrified, where the whole property resembled a landfill and you end up on TV threatened by a codes' enforcer. No, my father's brother, my favorite uncle, perhaps for already obvious reasons, a brilliant but failed medical student, "curated" as he constantly reminded us, a collection of preserved body parts of antiquity and other miscellaneous curiosities of taxidermy and wet specimens. It was weirdo hoarding at its best. He called it an innate gift of the bizarrely curious.

I grew up around all this. Archie's Traveling Odditorium was originally a backroad sideshow long before I was born, run by Archie and my dad's father, Archie Sr., but by the time I'd come around, what had been the dusty traveling museum was getting too large to manage. My grandfather was ailing and had settled the collection in the old Perkin's Boarding House here in Labortown. The size of the place was perfect to grow into. And did it ever. All Archie did was basically move into some of the back rooms and put a sandwich board out by the porch with the new hours. If he was home the place was open. If he was in the mood to sell something, he'd sell it. If not, then it was part of the "permanent collection."

Much of the place was immaculate, smelling of lab-grade cleanliness, with hints of formaldehyde and alcohol floating above it all like an invisible Frankenstein's lab mood. Lining the walls and several freestanding shelves were endless glass containers of all sizes full of specimens and taxidermy trophies. An unidentified head floating behind glass, a dried-up monkey hand holding a pinned World War II fragmentation grenade, a hammered copper and jewel-encrusted skull from Tibet, and a vial of Saint's blood housed in a shard of femur bone etched with Greek, were only a few of the special treats he'd found out in the world.

But his local collection was even more interesting. He had an oak-tree trunk full of cannon shot and bullet lead from the only skirmish in Labor County during the Civil War. The only known photograph of Oliver "Ollie" Howerton, the town founder, standing in a sea of hogs. A fully formed seven-foot-long, two-headed rattlesnake named The Lucifers, once the pride and joy of the snake-handling members of the Shaketown Hollow Holy Temple Church until one head bit the other during a tent revival in 1978.

And, of course, the full skeleton hanging from a stainless-steel frame in the middle of it all promised to me if I could keep my mouth shut about his most recent exciting acquisition: that cryogenic body tube. He'd gotten if from a bankrupting company out of Miami, by way of Louisville, by way of Harlan County. How it got to the mountains of southeast Kentucky, to our little city of Labortown, I don't think he ever really found out nor wanted to know.

It arrived intact, sealed, lights aglow with self-powered long-life battery.

I was crazy with the idea that something, *someone* might still be in it.

"You think . . . ?" I asked him.

"We'll find out this afternoon, won't we?" Uncle Archie teased, as we tugged it through the backloading doors of the house. It might have been on rollers, but it was still heavy for just the two of us. It felt like shoving around our Deepfreeze packed full of deer, bear, and turkey.

The guys that left it off were gone pretty quickly. They hadn't stuck around very long. They were in an old rental truck. The old logos were painted over, but still bleeding through. ELLER ICE CREAM was stenciled over everything. The driver had stayed in the driver's seat while the second man helped us drag the tube out of the back. Neither had uttered a word during the drop-off. The two men looked strangely alike. I didn't see any ice cream anywhere in the truck.

Uncle Archie was strict that no one but Dad and I could know about this, along with neighbor Jim. Me since I was a kid and never judged him much and was always asking questions and appreciated the weirdness going on, Dad since he was the official trustee of the home museum, and Jim because he was next door and also a 'Nam vet, and the only other person trustworthy enough to handle chain of command of the keys. Having only a few people with access to the collection was probably a good idea since for all we knew there really was a body in that freshly acquired cryogenic body tube in the back room from the soon defunct Chryo-Lab, LLC.

He'd been eyeing the company for a year before they'd finally flopped as a start-up. My uncle, along with 467 others, was scammed out of his investment of a thousand dollars for possible extended life. But he felt as though he had the last laugh when a mere fifteen hundred bucks through the hush-hush black-market oddities trade managed to locate and deliver to your home a cryotube, with or without a body, in less than two weeks, no questions asked.

It was all I could think about during mass at church that morning—the three of us, if neighbor Jim came over, standing around the hissing Deepfreeze of a thing, ready to pop the lid and see what was really inside. But my daydreams kept getting sidetracked to that Georgia bigfoot hoax some years ago where these guys had stuffed a gorilla suit full of a mess of opossum guts before freezing it all and claiming they'd found and preserved the elusive creature's carcass. A real Squatch body, finally. And some national Bigfoot hunters had supposedly paid good money for it before getting the thing tested. In the end, it just stunk of publicity.

Archie snuck out during the church service.

He was bad to do this, especially if he'd heard the sermon before. I didn't think much of it until after services were over and Dad told me we weren't getting to have our as-promised excitement.

"Archie's left town, son. He left me a voicemail."

"What?"

I was crushed.

"Just like that?"

"Yep. You know he's like that."

He was like that.

"That ain't fair."

It wasn't.

"Said he'd already checked that container. Told me to tell you we got all excited for nothing. It's empty. Nothing but frost in the thing. And some noxious fumes, so stay out of it."

I was so disappointed.

"He said to tell you he was sorry."

And mad. I wanted to be there when he opened it up, even if it was empty. I'd felt like it was something just for me and him to be in on. He'd cheated me.

"Said he'd be coming back from this trip with lots of new goodies, though."

He always did. He'd drop off the map for months, go who knows where, and return with loads of crazy stuff. Have lots of stories to tell. I loved him for that.

"Said for you to get with Jim for a set of keys."

"What for?" I asked.

"He's leaving you in charge."

So this was the day. Key access. So I couldn't be too mad at my uncle, could I? He'd traded me disappointment for responsibility. Up to then I'd only helped out. Given little tours. Helped with picking yard sales and flea markets for the occasional folk oddity. Conducted varmint control.

So I was left in charge, opening and closing the shop, in charge of the gift corner. But more than anything, I was to guard the treasury, including that cryotube in the walk-in closet out back, a special item no one but the select few even knew existed.

If there was a lull on a weekend I'd go back to check on the battery of that thing. I kept a chair by it. I'd sit in what was mostly dark, but for the few red and blue lights indicating the machine was active, still maintaining 215 degrees below zero inside, apparently for nothing at all.

But the question of *why keep it running* kept me curious. If Uncle Archie had opened it and found nothing, why keep it going so long after he'd left? Why keep it locked away? Why not display it? It would have brought a buck's worth of *ooh*s and *ahh*s for sure.

I admit I was tempted to pry the thing open more than once. What kid wouldn't be? But the idea of *what if* kept me at my word. Besides I had keys to the place now. Things were different. More was expected of me. I had to do more than just keep an eye on what I could see of the place, I figured. I was responsible for the mysteries, too.

So every time I'd notice the glowing red from the room, hear the low constant buzz from the room, I was reminded of what Uncle Archie would say occasionally when I'd ask too many questions: "There's things about the world we don't know, boy. Things seen. Some unseen. We have to live amongst them all."

I'd do just that. I'd wait.

The Hard Thing

Alder's final trip up the steps from the garage to his front porch was about all he had left in him. He hoisted the aged box of books with a grunt from waist level to atop the other three, making the stack about head height, the musty cardboard surprisingly sturdy and holding a half-hearted promise of balance. Smoke from the cigarette stub flapping in his lips was hot in his nose, threatening his eyes with sweat drops ready to river in and burn. He huffed, glad to be done with hauling books up the steps. Walked back to the comfort of his steel rocker. It was hot on his back, even in the shade, but it offered some rest. The day seemed out to cook him in his own fatigue.

He tried to rest, near motionless for a time he didn't bother tracking, sweat beading, trailing his temple, creeping along the curvature of his jaw and neck, soaking into the collar of the T-shirt he hadn't thought to change in at least two days, maybe more. Sure was nice not to care. The accumulating scent of self was comforting in a way. The sweat would dry, staining the cotton's cleanness, the acrid scent floating near his face like a reminder of the question he couldn't shake.

Until just now. Maybe the stink was doing him some good.

How many days was it since his father's first call, those words miring him down into such a loathsome mood? And how many calls since?

When you gonna finally be a man about things, son?

He'd never bothered asking himself such a question. It wasn't until things started really hurting that you finally reached a place in your head where you could have such a conversation. Where the walls of mirrors reflected past the internal bullshit. Where you can't lie to yourself.

A man is not a man until he believes himself one. That was his conclusion. He gave a nod of faint satisfaction and sipped his drink, arm bending slow at the elbow, glass offering up a last sip of precious sting, subtly toasting this simple moment of epiphany.

Wasn't that it? No magic, no ceremony. No snap of the finger in the imagined moment. The sudden wakefulness of maturity can't be legislated. Or taught, or beaten into someone. Men don't just wake up on an eighteenth birthday willing to vote and change their country. Or take responsibility for adult crimes. Don't willingly scurry like a hunted insect across fields with a friend's guts hanging from their soldiering equipment as the world explodes. He'd been there, on that field. It had only made him want to crawl back into childhood. Blood wasn't the answer.

His cell rang.

How's that vacation, son? his father's voice slurred. When wasn't it these days?

Why don't you use this time and find a real job, son?

His father had a simple and odd way of cutting to the painful quick. Alder robotically returned his regular humoring tone. This conversation, one they'd traded in endless versions, held nothing but the obligation of a dead-end ritual.

When you gonna finally be a man about things?

What a shitty thing to say to a son. He wanted to smash his fist through the phone, plow it in and stretch it across town full into his father's nosey smugness. Hurt him back. *I have real job, Dad,* Alder hissed into the face of the phone.

His father loved to remind him how so many others were out doing "real work" while him and his "associates" drank coffee, philosophized on stumps, and avoided the hardships of life, compliments of *real* men out doing *real* work at *real* jobs with *real* lives.

You'd feel better about yourself, all that money you waste, if you worked harder for it.

Money. Always about money. *And,* he added, securing the knife deeper, *you might have kept that family together. Sometimes doing the hard thing is what's best for a man.*

I've done things you can't even imagine, he wanted to tell him. *Worked harder than you know, than I'll ever privilege you with knowing.*

All Alder ever shared with his father about his time in the army was how boring it had been. How he was glad it was over. Only some of that was true.

Dad, I'm hanging up now.

Don't you hang up on me . . .

I'm hanging up.

When the realization finally hit it felt as if he'd wasted days becoming comfortable with something already sensed but ignored. It was a clear thing now, sitting there all along, obvious and waiting. You have to believe you're a man. The problem was, Alder didn't know what he believed anymore. Or whether the question even mattered.

The thought of calling his father up and screaming his conclusion over the phone crossed his mind. The temptation passed just as quickly, though. His father didn't expect an answer.

He squinted dry eyes, pulling in a scene identical to yesterday, sunlight heavy, building tops, mountain hues in a rippling midday heat. Loamy scent cooking up from thinning grass.

This replication was his vacation, away from his job over those hills, just far enough to be slightly disengaged, just close enough for it not to feel like a real break, a near workable false sense of safety in between. It was late June. For the fifth year he'd gone nowhere on his vacation.

But this year he was alone. Not just mentally, but physically alone and they were gone. Wife and daughter. Vacuumed out of his life by the self-destruct button he had slowly pressed for nearly ten excruciating years, watching the expanding destruction play out in frame-by-frame slow motion. And they'd stolen all the good air in the house, leaving nothing but an invisible dead space he couldn't shake.

He'd taken up sitting on the front porch a lot, avoiding inside, judging the time of day by the numbered mug of coffee and its temperature. By where he was in the day's pack of smokes and the yet emptied jar he used for an ashtray. By where the trees allowed sun to fall in the neglected garden flowers. By when his stomach growled and how long he could put off eating. By the honeyed line of bourbon in the bottle.

A corner of cardboard box gave and collapsed an inch, threatening to tumble across the porch and back down the steps. He stared them down, mentally daring them. He'd have to move them soon or risk it all making more of a mess than he had energy to care about.

But he dreaded having to be in the house. Something lurked inside, waiting to sneak up his back and choke him in his sleep. The sound of their names attached to everything still in there, claw-gripped and stubborn. Sleeping on the porch again sounded like a good idea.

The lecture seeded with him differently this time, not by way of new words, but by some chance of timing, the new ring of truth maybe digging deeper into his vulnerability. Against better judgment, his days were spent questioning not only how he made a living, but his adulthood. This led to questioning other things and by the end of the first week he'd effectively chipped up the foundation of everything he was—and wasn't. Every choice, hesitation.

He'd scraped himself completely out. It hurt. Especially while there alone and drunk most of the time. There was little freeing about it. The more he thought the more he folded in on himself. His sitting spells lasted longer, his mind racing enough to make up for his lack of movement.

He just didn't want to go into the house. Alder, the monster, lived in there.

Something was in there dying. He could smell it.

What was left of them was in there. As if memories had scents. Everyone knows they do.

He would eventually have to go in.

He glanced around, taking painful stock of his surroundings. Wife: gone. Daughter: gone. House: nearly the bank's. Car: falling apart. Yard: out of control. Cats: somewhere. Inside the house: electricity, left cut off after missing the bill last month. Upstairs: a bed he avoided. No wonder the porch was more inviting.

Boxes. Boxes everywhere. Half-packed, half-unpacked, spilled about with no real method. Floor: books, stacked and unread. Tabletops: covered in loose files and scribble-covered paperwork. Bookshelves: overflowing. Books were one thing he hadn't grown up around, a mystery finally stumbled across in college. Now, they were everywhere. When they got in the way, they became tabletops, towering shaky skyscrapers in corners. Most were read. Some not. They felt cumulative, a decades-long chronology of self-centered escapism. A retreat haven, a silent collection he likened unto damming back his father's scorn of his professional life.

But wasn't riding a desk better than riding a bird? Hanging out the side of a chopper? With the "God Gun" strapped to you? You and the machine. One thing. Killing from above. Death from above. Special delivery. Uncle Sam and your father send their best.

He drew a loud and long breath, feeling like he'd forgotten how, stretched the pulse of blood back into his arms and legs, propped the door open and grabbed a box of books.

The cats shot through his legs. He'd given up caring whether they were in or out.

The heaviness was there as he walked in, like a special indoor shadow knowing only his form, searching him in that instant. No book would carry away such a spatial loathing. No too-loud music would drown the burden of utter, shapeless guilt wrapping him up, his ex-wife's words rolling out in his own voice. A whispered bawling, animal-like.

Why . . . why? I'm so lonely . . . she'd cried out over the phone a week after they'd left town.

The strange sound from his lips would trail off, leaving him wideeyed and wide mouthed, fading wordless in response, no one left to hear his sorry mumbled excuses for having no excuse.

I don't have the answer, Annie.

Her name hadn't crossed his lips in weeks. He killed off the word, surprised as the warm bottle met his mouth. He'd forgotten bringing it in. The day's dregs at the bottom found his tongue, seared her name clean.

He caught a shot of himself in the last mirror he hadn't broken in the house.

Ain't I just like you? he whispered at the image. Alcoholic breath wafting back at him from the foggy glass.

Light failed. The floor snapped as he stumbled his paces through rooms, the evening roaming about in slow chase, soon nearly too dark for shadows. He was busy now, even in the lightlessness, his father's advice driving him to the evening's task, intent, unafraid finally, something having given, collapsed, exhausted with arguing against a full intoxication. The curtains pulled. Windows shut. Front and back doors bolted.

Time passed. As misery will in the dark. Motionless. Shifting. The mind a wreck at sea.

Then he was in the living room on the floor staring into the lit fireplace, as he always was these late, late nights. But this time a brilliant, uncomfortably hot fire glowed. It had been one of summer's hottest days and the house's air was off with no electricity. He was stuffing as many books as the fireplace could stand, his mind fuzzed with so many slugs of bourbon sloshing in his gut.

He'd carried more books into the living room, finally emptying the library after several nights, adding to that the garage's books from this day's work, and now he'd surrounded himself, fort-like, with massive piles of pieces of his life. Books, files stuffed with old work notes, journals, stacks of bills and junk mail from the months. He sat cross-legged in the middle of the room facing the destructive and angry mouth of the fireplace, his limbs and head heavy from the alcohol, barely able to concentrate by now, the heat quickly drying his sweaty shirt. It was soon a furnace, filled with loud amassed flames licking up the chimney, the glow lighting only his space, the house fully gone to night.

The fireplace was overstuffed, purposefully. As a little space opened, he tossed more in, prodded in more with an iron tool, a book, a file, a journal, a handful of mail, the heat growing near unbearable, stinging and tightening the skin of his arms and face. The lack of temptation to page through each book surprised him, the desire was gone for some symbolic reminder of the pleasure they'd provided. No hesitation to dwell for a moment on a memory held in a journal's passage. In they went. Up the chimney, ash by ash. He made sure to toss several books in at a time so he could watch the spines, the titles cracking into black. The first books were morphing to black layered ash and collapsing under the shifting denseness, alive, pancaking down, spitting sparks and leaking glowing smoke out of the corners of the fireplace up into the living room ceiling.

The greedy weight fell in on itself finally, toppling layers out and licking yellow and red, new air igniting the fire's innards. Alder watched in some kind of crazed expectation as the nearest piles caught, lighting the room in living shadows of red and black. The room filled with smoke faster than he'd expected.

He had a hope. To have at least a few moments of clarity, some magic in the act. Even as blind-drunk as he'd managed. He remained as motionless as he could stand, cross-legged still, testing the crawling heat curling his arm hair. He could smell the rubber of his tennis shoes smoldering.

Something screamed upstairs. The smoke detector. The flames fingered out closer to his lap, stalking him a page at a time, a cover at a time, a story at a time. Year by year. By passage. Line and word. He struggled in keeping his watering eyes open. The dam of smoke burst toward him, around him. He stared through, past the brightness barreling in his face. He forced his eyes wide, refusing to blink, fought the fear of the heat, afraid of missing something in the flames, a sign boiling from all the charring and flighted ink in the roiling mess. He heard the growling ball of fire starting to crunch down around him and finally eat into the remaining circle of books.

Keep staring.

Was that something there?

Keep staring.

Or there?

Keep staring...

But there was nothing of interest in the flames. Nothing in the pain. Nothing in the light. No fantastic answer from the crisped words around him swirling up in little tornadoes of vanishing black.

So he gave in. Lightheaded. Vision tunneling.

Expelled his used air and moaned with disappointment, in recognition of what he'd done.

He gasped in the anticipated poisoning black ash breath, felt a seizing in his lungs, the quick bursting choke, tasted the deep smoke.

His lips trembled some semblance of words no one would see.

Riding Shotgun
with Dory

We'd spend as much time out on the porch as we could stand. Especially in the spring. If the sun traveled just right along the tin roof's edge it wouldn't get in our eyes all day long and Papaw and I could sit and rock from morning up to evening if we could swing it, never even go inside if we didn't have a good reason. Like it was some sort of contest, waiting each other out. Mamaw would bring us sandwiches, and cookies, and something to drink if it looked like one us was about to break. And if the evenings were mild enough and the mosquitoes weren't too starved, you could fall asleep on Mamaw's steel sled rocker and not wake up all night. Let the birds wake you when the sun came up. Do it all over again if you felt like it.

Those kinds of days alone were reason enough to love staying with them. It was a different place than home. Like slipping on another world for a kid like me. Visiting my grandparents got me away from down in town, from my parents' over-watchful eyes for a weekend. For longer on summer breaks. Everything a rotten kid like me wanted was up on Long Grace Mountain.

I only felt weird about staying when Papaw—that was mom's dad—was getting out of his head, which I didn't understand so much back then. I only thought he was a strange "old timer" as dad called him. Dad didn't go up the mountain much. I wasn't old enough to fully catch on to what all the nervous whispers meant, all the rough settling down they had to do with Papaw sometimes, how he'd get so upset over nothing and start yelling. But he was never like that with me.

Sometimes he'd wander off. Get lost for a day or two. I believed most of their fibs about him being off visiting friends somewhere. But they quit talking to me about his "visits" once I got wise and asked how just visiting friends would cause him to get a pant leg ripped off his overalls and have so many briar scratches all over his long arms and legs, all over his gaunt face. I'd settled with stories such as him wrestling a rabid coyote off the back of his friend's prize heifer, though a month later he'd have changed it to a territorial dispute between two sizeable groundhogs. It was easy to imagine Papaw wrestling a wild animal. He always seemed so strong to me. He towered over me, tall and lanky. He'd say, "Catch up, I'm gonna lap ya!" when we were out checking the fence lines.

It was strange to negotiate those times, like we were all tip-toeing on a crate of freshly laid eggs. The air around those visits was hard to breathe a little. That's the way I remember it being.

But most of the time things were just fine and I was happy to be there.

It was an old hilly farm almost an hour from Labortown, but still in the county. It was only fifteen miles away, but drop a little farm way up in the mountains, accessible with poor secondary state roads full of break-neck hairpin turns, add 750 feet of elevation, and that's why it took so long to get there. It was a mix of isolation and paradise, settled by Mamaw's grandfather just before the Civil War was on. When I'd asked about battles nearby she said they were so far up in the hills the war hardly touched them. She guessed it must have been too far to march for nothing.

That didn't keep me from imagining the war making its way up the valley, though, and over the farm's rolling hills. I'd be all over the property, with Buck the black lab at my side, exploring everything not nailed down as Mamaw used to say.

I'd be a Union spy watching the farm from a distance. Or a Confederate officer holding my men in line, marching over the hills to engage the enemy headfirst into point-blank cannon fire. Or a crack shot Union cavalry sniper in the trees taking out rebel officers. I'd prowl through Papaw's barn and old storage and work buildings, scrounging for what the men back at garrison needed for the coming bad weather.

When I got tired of roleplaying as a soldier, I'd veer off into my other obsessions, like UFO investigating or survivalist field-expedient trapping. I'd read every book in the town library on Project Blue Book, so I figured I knew what I needed about alien visitations and unidentified objects in the sky. I more than once tried to hoax Papaw into calling a meeting of the Long Grace Mountain residents about the intricate crop circles I'd stomped out in his grazing field. The only problem was that I'd carried out my missions at night without light and ended up with indecipherable zig-zags and swirls.

"Looks like them aliens of yours were drinking before they landed here, huh?" was all he said, but he'd go along with the routine and take soil samples along with me to take back to town.

I had the run of the old place. And it had the run of my young mind.

Papaw was a leatherworker for years. To me, his workshop was a castle of amazement. Though I wasn't supposed to, I'd get into there as often as I could, especially in the mornings. I'd creep in as light made way through the splitting slats of wood siding, the old wormy chestnut milled from the farm, motes streaming in, all of it enough to barely see by. It was enough to spook me by at least. It was a ghostly place. I could smell the old, unfinished hides before wriggling myself through a larger hole in the backend of the building. It was sweet and musty. He kept thick sawdust on the floor, spongy to the step. Things lived in there and shifted and bolted as I'd worm through the angles of the place. It felt like a large organism of hide and oil, wood and hardware, curing in some mostly hibernating state, but dreaming about springing to full life with me in it, to extend its crawlers and eyes and march off the hills down into civilization to wreck its havoc.

Papaw'd been skilled enough, especially once he'd retired from the knife works, to make all manner of goods to sell at the flea markets and festivals for the extra cash they needed. Everything from knife sheathes to custom belts, utility work straps, and even fine slaughter aprons for the more fashion-conscious meat-house employees. You should have seen the purses he could make from good hog leather.

His specialty, however, was toddler-sized miniature saddles you could strap to a large dog or such sized animal. Talk about cornering the market. As far as anyone knew, Papaw was the only one around making these. Of course, he made them far too cheaply. If he'd been savvy, and wasn't scared of "them internet things," he'd have made the whole family rich. Comfortable, at least.

Now understand these weren't the same as miniature pony saddles, which were commoner and not very exciting. His version was smaller, perfectly sized for dogs like Buck the lab. They'd even fit goats, sheep, and medium hogs if you wanted such foolishness. The key was his skill with fashioning the saddle sturdy enough not to fail, but light enough not to burden the animal and get PETA called on him.

The toddler version wasn't so light as to work with the largest turkeys on the farm, however. He'd learned this the hard way. I had

too, supposedly. Papaw told me once, "It's easy to make saddles for
dogs and goats and less stubborn pigs. But you ever heard tale of a
turkey saddle?

I hadn't.

"Exactly," he said, softening up a new piece of hide he'd picked
up in town, shaping it, glancing up at plans he'd sketched on a
sheet of paper he had tacked on the workshop wall. I could see the
gears turning in his mind. "It was a short-lived dream, young'n."

He'd quit with the saddles for a while. Mamaw said it was
mostly due to him being sick, though I don't remember him ever
having a cold as long as I knew him. But he was back with a vengeance with this new idea.

I'd sit and watch him for hours. I was fascinated with the tools
and his hands, the work, how naturally he knew what to reach for
without glancing to where all his hardware waited. The punches,
knives, shears, and mallets were like extra parts of his hands, additional hands even. When he was finished with the first attempt he
showed it to me. It was strangely adapted to a turkey's body, a thin-
ner make, strapped to accommodate the rounder male's heavier
and stouter body and avoiding the wings. It was obvious no toddler
was fitting such a tiny saddle. I mentioned that.

"No shit," Papaw said. "You ever looked at the tiny sticks turkeys walk on for legs?"

He had a point.

"A drumstick might be meaty, but they got skinny calves and
ankles that can snap like twigs. We need some experimenting to
figure out a baseline first."

And boy did he have some specimens to experiment on around
the farm. I don't know what Mamaw was feeding them, but a few
were monstrous huge. I think they'd bred theirs with the wild turkeys that roamed around the forest. Or maybe with the wild boars,
I don't know. The birds roosted along the tree lines of the farm and

never seemed to wander off very far. They were a hardy and mean bunch of birds, half-wild themselves. I never got too close, afraid of getting chased.

Papaw had a favorite bird that seemed pretty tame to be so potentially mean. El Dorado was this monster tom's name. I'd watched it fight off two starving coyotes, so I knew it was the real deal as far as strength and sass goes, skinny ankles and all. Its spurs were an inch long and he was pushing every bit of thirty pounds. It would follow Papaw or Mamaw around like lap dog hungry for attention. I think they fed it high-protein puppy treats.

I could tell Papaw was excited something awful.

"Too bad you ain't younger like you used to be, young'n," he said over supper one Saturday night, finally letting loose with the mystery of the short-lived, toddler-riding turkey story.

"You were the right size when you were just short of two years old. I'd say we owe you about half the small fortune we made off those saddles we sold, don't you think so, honey?"

He winked at Mamaw.

"Him riding Old Enoch at the fairs sold every saddle I had. You'd pull in quite a crowd."

"I don't remember any of that, Papaw," I protested.

I did remember just a little, of course, but never enough to know if he was telling the truth. The details of things changed with every telling around that place.

"Oh, you wouldn't you were so young, young'n. I could lift you with one finger."

Mamaw glared. I could never tell how much he was making up, if she was complicit in his tales, or if she'd just never liked him exploiting me.

"Who was Old Enoch?"

"Shoot! Only the biggest tom turkey ever in the state is what Enoch was!" Papaw crowed, flapping his arms bent at the elbows and shoving his head forward with pursed lips meant to resemble a beak. He could have been imitating a rooster, too.

"A forty-three-pound state-fair champion he was! You rode that beast like a little champion yourself."

"Until he turned on you," Mamaw chimed in, sounding disgusted.

It got quiet. Papaw turned grim. Mamaw even stopped chewing.

"He tossed you in the middle of a ride. In front of everyone."

More silence.

"I won't abide such orneriness," Papaw said, even grimmer.

Mamaw stared like she didn't know what else would come out of his mouth.

"Enoch was like a son to me." His voiced cracked a little.

She rolled her eyes and started back eating her mashed potatoes.

"But we had fresh turkey that night for supper, huh, honey? Froze the rest of his ass and had him for Thanksgiving two years in a row. I won't abide no orneriness from no damn animal."

"Old Enoch was tough," Mamaw added. "Took forever to bake."

Papaw just shook his head. I couldn't tell if he was upset or laughing. He excused himself to the front porch to smoke his pipe.

"Mamaw, I thought turkey's ankles were too skinny to carry a kid."

She giggled at that.

"Well, you were a puny little thing, too, honey. And Enoch was no ordinary creature. I really don't blame Henry for being so mad. That turkey about tore your back off it flogged you so bad."

Every time I'd brought up the scars I still had on my back, my mother never wanted to talk much about them. I guess she'd been mad as hell at Papaw over the whole turkey accident. I remember her yelling at him that he'd have made more money with such a dangerous animal fighting him with other deranged beasts than strapping a poor toddler to the back of it who couldn't say no.

Papaw eventually ran back into house. We were washing up the dishes.

"Honey! I got it! Young'n, don't fret, I figured out what we're gonna do!"

He grabbed the portable phone and took it out on the front porch and I could hear him having a long, excited conversation until the sun was well down.

Arnie Lowman was on the front porch with Papaw by early the next morning. Mamaw told me to leave them alone for a bit. That once they got together no telling what might come of the day. Arnie was a widower from another mile across the mountain, and though a buddy of Papaw's from way back, they'd been rivals for Mamaw's hand back in the day. But they'd gotten past that, mostly. Arnie liked to flirt still. He just wasn't very good at it. Or very subtle. When he tried it wasn't enough to even make Mamaw blush. She'd just shake her head and feel sorry for him, I guess.

He had a habit of bringing her flowers he'd pick from his farm, but he walked everywhere he couldn't thumb a ride to, and hand carried the flowers. They'd be a wilted mess by the time he arrived. He'd been better off picking flowers out of Mamaw's own garden and handing them over. At least they'd have stood a chance.

I was inside busting a gut about what they were up to out there. I wanted to be out on the porch with the men. I could hear leather slapping around. Clanking metal. Low mumbling. Heavy boots on the porch floorboards. The dog barking. They were amused with each other's stories, chuckling. Plans were in the making.

"El Dorado! Ellll—Do-raaaaa-do! Yip, yip, yip!"

This I'd heard before, Papaw calling up the big tom from the forest. I suspected they were experimenting with the turkey saddle. And me inside.

Then—"Dory! Heeeeere, Dory!"

Now who the heck was this Dory, I wondered. Another turkey? Arnie's dog? I couldn't stand it anymore.

"Mamaw! I'm going out now!" I took off for the porch before I heard her respond one way or the other.

I spied out the screen door. Dory was no turkey. No dog. Now I'd seen squirrels before. Who hasn't? But the squirrel tearing across the front yard toward Arnie was the reddest and fluffiest and biggest one I'd ever seen. It was carrying an acorn in each fist, its cheeks chock-full, and it was half running, half hopping full out on its hind legs. It scampered up the porch steps and onto Arnie's lap and popped all those acorns into the man's overall pocket then hopped up on his shoulder and settled down into what looked like its usual resting place. Not a second later, El Dorado let out the loudest gobble I'd ever heard and came flapping down off a limb from the tree line and started strutting his stuff across the front yard, parting a gaggle of chickens pecking in the dirt. He was a body taller than most of them.

"Boy, come on out here. I can hear you."

I obeyed, eyes wide.

"Ever met Arnie?"

"Hi."

"Ever met Dory?"

I stared at the squirrel. It stared at me with round, nonblinking, black eyes. It felt like the creature was accessing my thoughts. I looked away.

Arnie laughed. "Yep, she reads minds. Better watch out. Shake hands, Dory."

The squirrel leaned out its face, nose twitching, and extended a tiny arm and paw. I hesitated. Its jerky moves creeped me out.

"Go ahead. This is the best-trained fox squirrel in that state. Took best in show at the state fair two years in a row."

I reached and shook its paw with my thumb and pointer finger.

Papaw had grabbed El Dorado by now. I admit he had a way with the bird. He was strapping the new saddle he'd been working on over the back the bird. The saddle, about four inches wide and five inches long, fit across the bird's back with two custom billets and cinches, one low along the breast in front of the wings and one behind the wings and up under the behind. Though aggravated, the bird held mostly still and allowed him to work the webbing around its big round body. He never flapped his wings or tried to spur Papaw's face off. Or, El Dorado, being a possible relative of Enoch, might have heard tell how Papaw dealt with ornery little screwballs around the farm.

Arnie stood and walked off the porch to where Papaw and El Dorado were in the middle of the dirt yard, the squirrel still on his shoulder. I followed. I put two and two together before long. I knew what was about to happen.

Mamaw was standing quietly in the door, drying her hands with a dishrag, shaking her head. She must have known what was coming, too.

Arnie crouched near the bird, his head even with its jerky head.

"Y'all get ready to clear back. I ain't thought much of this part through," Papaw warned.

Now the dirt road out of the holler was pocked with holes. They were filled with soupy water most of the time. The water would come off the hills and rut out the road and the run-off would stick around in the potholes, breeding bugs and whatnot. Since there were no significant creeks nearby, these spots out in the road attracted all manner of animals for watering.

Things would pass away on the road, too. Mostly opossums. This would attract a turkey vulture or two. Or three. Nothing incensed El Dorado more than a vulture in his territory. He'd fight them all day for free.

At this very moment, fifty yards down the road, gaggling up around some craters of fetid water, was a crew of vultures snacking on something that was a week's worth of ripe. They'd probably swooped in under the trees all quiet rather than shown themselves in their usual swirling premeal death thermal. As far as they knew, things were all fine on the buffet front.

Arnie lowered his hand down to the horn of that saddle, thereby turning his arm into a miniature ramp. About the time Dory was halfway down Arnie's arm headed for the saddle, my little brain caught up with Papaw and Arnie's grand Saturday afternoon project.

I'd never heard a turkey growl before. I'll never forget the sound. Every feather on that animal shivered with the resonance of that warning grumble.

In my head I yelled, *Shit!* but I was smart enough not to shout it out loud, especially anywhere near Mamaw. Papaw and Arnie yelled it loud enough for them and me.

None of us could move fast enough. Dory was on that saddle, her little paws latched on the horn, legs bowed and clamped. I guess the idea was to break El Dorado for future rides. Papaw caught a spur across the shin first and gave out a wild howl and set to hopping in pain. Arnie got caught broadways across the face, the feathers scratching his eyeballs and near blinding him.

I glanced over my shoulder, scared of how close the danger might be to me, and saw poor Dory flapping around like a determined rag doll barely holding on, but being a trooper for the cause. The bird wasn't having it and was trying to flap away. Dory probably topped out at two-and-a-half pounds, so that alone wasn't keeping the turkey on the ground, but Dory flopping around from side to side interfered with El Dorado's wing coordination. All he could manage was an unorganized flapping and a good sprint trying to get a head of steam enough to take to the open sky.

They both passed me up close on the left, which was fine if it meant I wasn't getting stripped of flesh. Mamaw shouted for me to duck. "Duck, Jimmy!" I crouched as feathers swiped my neck and hair.

Papaw and Arnie were yelling at their animals to come back and giving chase.

"El Dorado!"

"Dory!"

The turkey was out the front gate and in the road getting its bearings when it up and halted. The squirrel was resting with its head down, breathing heavier than most squirrels do even with their fast hearts. Dory's busy tail wasn't even bolting around like usual. It appeared that El Dorado, who I tended to call "El D" when he was in fighting mode, had spotted something. He let out what I knew was his best "who the hell are you and why are you in my area" gobbles. In answer, we all heard the unmistakable cackle and hiss of a turkey vulture times, say, ten. That awful sound sent chills down my back.

El D was gone. Out of sight down the road like a vapor trail. With Dory right with him like she was riding into the gates of hell and glory. That turkey would defend his territory if it killed him and Dory.

Papaw saw what was happening and hollered to Mamaw. She'd seen it too.

"Get my shotgun, baby!"

Mamaw was already on the move. She despised a vulture. She had his double-barrel, duel-triggered, breakdown, twelve-gauge shotgun already loaded in no time and tossed it to him off the porch. I'd never seen the two of them move so fast. It was like they'd done practice drills. Arnie was right by Papaw, gazing up at Mamaw with loving eyes, probably falling back fully in love with her at that very moment even if his corneas were all scratched up.

They turned, now armed for bear, and vulture, to defend their extended furry family. About that time, El D and Dory were beating retreat back to the fort with at least a half dozen vultures in pursuit. It was a terrible racket. El D must have left an impressive body count down the road because these birds looked to be veering down on Dory as a replacement dessert they'd missed. Our bird was running and flapping and hopping so hard he was leaving a trail of feathers in the vultures' faces. Dory by now had either caught on to the hang of riding, broke El D, or they'd just joined forces in agreement to save their own hides. She was in full stride as though she was born in the saddle. The vultures were snipping at El D's tail and scrawny ankles and spitting feathers and salivating over what fresh turkey with a side of squirrel would taste like, no doubt.

The lead pursuer wouldn't find out. His ugly head turned to a red mist in the mountain wind when Papaw wasted him with the first round. I wasn't expecting it and screamed out, falling to my knees out of the way. Even El D ducked in surprise, but kept running.

Papaw walked in his assault a few steps and squeezed off the next cocked trigger, winging two more birds with the spread shot. He was standing tall, like a hero in battle. He elbowed the gun with a loud snap, the spent rounds popping out with a trail of smoke. He'd reloaded in no time.

Click. Click. The triggers cocked. Gun raised and sighted. Mamaw yelling out suddenly. A new warning. "Watch out, Henry! They're turning!"

The whole mess of birds, plus the squirrel leaning into the change of direction, had turned and was headed for the front porch now. Straight for Papaw and Arnie. And me. And Mamaw.

One shot rang out and the front yard filled with another explosion and jet of smoke. Everything rattled. Feathers and a splatter of blood smacked me on the face. My ears rang. Mamaw screamed.

Another shot. The same carnage. Arnie screamed this time. Fur flew.

Papaw dropped the shotgun in the dirt.

Gigantic birds—what ones left fit to escape within a thin feather of their mangy lives—were taking flight up the mountain slope.

El Dorado lay motionless, bleeding out in the dirt.

Dory was mostly unscathed, but was flapping about in some pain from the single pellet lodged in her left eye socket. Arnie, the gentleman that he was, would later fashion her up the nicest lace eyepatch you've ever seen on a squirrel.

Another vulture lay dead.

Papaw had fired off the two rounds about as blindly as one could in the fog of war. He reported later that he'd suffered a flashback when all the birds had turned and come at everybody in what he'd described as a "red wave." I was confused by that since he'd never been in combat before.

I left that evening and didn't go back to stay with my grandparents for a long while. I couldn't understand it at the time, but Papaw needed a break. When I did go back, it wasn't so much for seeing them as it was to make sure the El D fiasco didn't end up being my final memory of the place. Mamaw and Mom took Papaw for a little vacation somewhere that evening. Somewhere, Mamaw said, where there weren't no vultures, or state fair champion turkeys, or leather tools. Just some rest and relaxation. Somewhere down in town off Long Grace Mountain.

Uncle Archie's Underground Reunion

The whole family was mad as hell after getting the wool pulled over our eyes by that fancy photographer, Johnny G. Porter. But Uncle Archie was a little too greedy for a quick infusion of cash for what he anticipated would be the coming summer's rush of tourism activity. He couldn't help but bite and that Porter man only had to yank the line after a good teasing. Who'd turn down free publicity?

Porter was a famous mountain-life photographer. At least he thought so. He just showed up one day, all dressed up in what we assumed was famous photographing clothes—a dress shirt and skinny tie, beady little sunglasses, and a netted fishing vest with more pockets than I'd ever seen on a piece of fashion. He tossed photography terminology around, of course, like *aperture* and *depth of field* and "stand still for heaven's sake." And he had two big impressive cameras weighing down his neck. Two. I guess in case one ran out of wind.

He was talking up a storm about how excited he'd been after hearing about our famous Underground Reunion, one of the more popular attractions here at Archie's Odditorium & Gifts (if it's been a while since you came by, we've added a corner for

souvenirs so visitors can take a little reminder home with them).
Before Uncle Archie up and vanished on a treasures acquisition
trip two years ago, he'd worked for almost five years on what can
only be described as a miniature hybrid of the burial catacombs of
Paris and the Capuchin mummy vaults of Italy, created mostly of
leftover Kentucky Fried Chicken scrap bones, dried and shrunken
apple doll heads carved in the shape of skulls and zombies, and discarded doll and toy parts. If such a sight doesn't get you to pile the
wife, or husband, and kids into the station wagon and drive at least
three counties over for a look-see, what would, right?

This Porter fella talked a good game. Had us believing his pro-
posed photo essay had all the potential for getting a wider exposure
than what got him on the photography map in the first place: The
Kentucky Blue People Coal Union Strike of '84. None of us had
heard of such a thing, but Uncle Archie said that if there were blue
people in Kentucky he'd make a note to go find them and bring
back some collectibles.

He claimed he'd get us on the "Appalachian map." I googled
that and told him all I could find was "Maps of Appalachia" and
that most of the videos I pulled up pronounced *Appalachia* like we
did, not the way he did, like he was saying *Apple-Asia*. He claimed
he didn't have time to explain what he meant, nor his accent, to
a kid.

The entrance to the Underground Reunion was a stoop door
just off the gift-shop corner. A self-guided tour only cost a dollar.
A guided tour was another fifty cents. And that extra fifty cents
was worth it, if you ask me.

I'd had numerous responsibilities through the years, especially
when I was too young to argue. Before we had lights run down
there, Uncle Archie had rigged up a stationary bike generator.
He'd have me on that thing peddling at just the right speed to
keep the lights going. If they dimmed too much in the middle of

a tour, he'd yell out, "Peddle, Boy! Peddle! I ain't losing another customer down here!" That worried the tourists occasionally, but it wasn't anything to really worry about. We never lost anyone. Uncle Archie even had me make up a chalkboard. *Guests lost on tour so far: None.* Porter took a bunch of shots of me standing by the board by the entrance giving the two thumbs-up.

The tour was simple, but effective. The tunnel zig-zagged back about thirty feet. Uncle Archie couldn't dig a straight line, I guess. It all ended in a large round room. Much of the walls were lined vertical with barn slats or roughly cut poles. It felt like a coal-mine shaft, some told us. Shelves of the homemade art lined the walls. Uncle Archie fancied himself a kind of Dr. Frankenstein when it came to piecing odd things together. Thank god we all loved KFC. He'd create new animals out of bones he'd salvage from bucket meals mixed with carcasses he'd find on the side of the road. Some of the creatures he put together were nightmarish. Ever seen a coyote skull on a turkey vulture body? With a cowboy squirrel riding the thing?

He claimed to have done the math and bragged that after burning through so many four-inch glue sticks, he'd used enough to string them from Labortown to Lexington, if he took the freeway.

Much of the tunnel was outfitted with doll bodies fitted with dried-apple doll heads carved in the shape of skulls. This is actually how the whole idea for the Underground Reunion came about in the first place. Uncle Archie accidently discovered you could fashion dried up skulls from apples instead of little old women and men noggins. He'd tried his hand at some apple doll faces one weekend when things were slow in the shop and set them up to dry. By the time they'd dried out and shrunk, the eyes were too large and sunken back and their noses were caved in. He hadn't bothered googling how cut them up properly. Within a month, given his tendency for obsessions, he'd carved a hundred of them and had them up drying for a "project" he hadn't figured out yet.

By spring we'd moved the special taxidermy section of the larger shop out from behind the counter and he'd torn a door through the wall and accessed the unfinished bunker he'd started at the height of the Cold War. That part of the building was butted right up against the hill. None of us knew what was behind the wall. He even had a short ribbon-cutting ceremony for just us before giving us all flashlights and saying, "C'mon in, y'all. Nobody was home last time I checked."

We thought he'd up and become a prepper suddenly, but after he'd shared his vision of the Underground Reunion, we all chipped in just to see if anything came of it. Apparently he'd toured the Paris catacombs when he was younger. These are ancient mining tunnels under the city filled with the remains of millions of Parisians. The skeletal remains were transported from the overloaded aboveground mass graves over decades, the skulls and long bones arranged into some of the most macabre assemblages of death art on the planet. As for the Italian Capuchin monks, they were famous for doing more or less the same in their crypts, often with full mummified corpses of brethren and the local deceased.

My uncle dreamed about us having our own tiny version of this weirdness as a side ticket item to the oddities store. He called it the Underground Reunion. It was like visiting all your dead mummified ancestors, if you were no more than two-foot tall.

Another section was nothing but hanging baby dolls painted up with Voodoo skull faces. He'd spent some time in New Orleans, too. Imagine that. One of my jobs early on was to bury all the dolls to hurry up that uglified vintage feel to them. The problem was keeping up with where all the little mass graves were and preventing our curious dogs from coming in behind me and excavating the lose piles of fresh clay. By the time we pulled them out, they looked perfectly ancient and creepy. Some were hung upside down by the ankles. Some the wrists. One shelf was nothing but fractured porcelain heads stacked in little cairn pyramids. One section might be lined only with arms or legs, another with limbless torsos painted yellow, red, or white. It was a mess, but an artistic one. One part he was particularly proud of was how he'd arranged painted doll arms along a wooden plant to spell out TUrN BACK.

Outfitting it with so many dolls was easy. At first, Uncle Archie sent me out with a ten dollar bill every Saturday afternoon during peak yard-sale season. My record was seventeen good-sized dolls in one day. I never told him I found that bunch in a sack by the trash bin at Sandy's Thrift Store. Once people caught on to what we were putting together, mysterious boxes of donations appeared out on the road by the mailbox. My job was to cull through them. Imagine that, us being picky we had so much junk to choose from.

We sometimes fastened a few of the apple skulls to big human-looking roots of ginseng and manroot. He'd painted names and dates of births and deaths on some of the larger apple heads like how skulls in those European crypts were dated, which wasn't easy since apples usually shrunk up to less than half the original size.

We tried carving lots of types of apples. The everyday varieties from the stores shrunk up way too small, limiting the size of bodies we could put the heads on, though the end product was weird looking. But when Uncle Archie happened upon the Japanese Hokuto, the world-record-holding apple for size, he was down at Carley Johnson's hometown grocery the next morning filling out an order and feeling pretty optimistic. They weren't cheap, and we didn't stick to carving them forever, but the largest ones you'll see in there are those Japanese ones. Carly told us once that if it hadn't been for us special ordering so many crates of Hokuto apples, he'd have folded up his business during the fruits and vegetable crash of '08.

While we regretted it, all the shrunken skull-apple head art had to eventually be placed off-limits with stapled wire screen. Besides keeping all the bodies upright and securely stacked like so many of the Capuchin monks are displayed in their creepy restive states, the screens helped keep people from leaving with a little souvenir. But most importantly, the screens deterred the giant tunneling rats from stealing and eating the heads from our bunker. They were voracious little bastards.

We learned the hard way at first, losing a lot of art to the mystery. The animals would burrow in and grab the bodies by the tasty head and drag them off for feasting. We were puzzled until an overly jealous juvenile rat choked to death on an apple head one night. The gagging ruckus echoing through the tunnel woke Uncle Archie up. Mystery solved. He started peppering the heads with a little rat poison and coating them with an eighth inch of shellac. Any rat determined enough to chew on one after that deserved what it got. Broken teeth and death.

There was a time, though, when I was appointed "Tunnel Rat, Master of Catacombs Preservation." I was thirteen and just short enough to get around in the bunker without hunching over or turning sideways. "We could have used you up near the Cambodian border, boy," Uncle Archie told me. "They practically lived in tunnels up there. No wonder we couldn't find them."

One morning we heard the varmints in there whooping up a good old time and having their way with our hard work. Uncle Archie'd had enough. He left and came back with a pump-action pellet gun and a pair of night-vision goggles he claimed he'd won in a card game off a Russian boxer back when he'd visited Laos, handed me the items, refused to peddle the bike generator, and sent me into the long dark. "Takes a Tunnel Rat to kill tunnel rats," he said, thinking that sounded like encouragement to a young teenager about to get eaten slowly by vermin. I killed seven of the bastards before I was bit on the ankle and retreated. He said that was a good start as he counted them in the front yard. He had them lined up head-to-head as if the living ones would see and spread the word.

"Yeah! Go tell your VC friends about *Operation Rotten Apple Core*!" he'd screamed into the dark opening. I asked dad what a "VC" and a "Tunnel Rat" was, but he only shook his head and mumbled something about "PTSD," and too much "Agent Orange," which I also didn't know anything about.

Porter liked that story a lot. Had me hold a BB gun at the ready and clamp a knife in my teeth like a pirate and walk out of the dark of the tunnel. He told me that shot would definitely make the story. So he had the run of the place for two days. Made all sorts of promises, taking notes on our stories about the store, our lives, taking shots of us around the shop. But it all went fishy when he had me take off my shoes and smear my face and hands with a little dirt and posed me sitting on the front porch steps of the store.

"We got plenty of running water," I told him.

"And this parking lot gravel hurts my bare feet," I complained, as he posed me by one of Uncle Archie's rusted-out antique cars.

"It's all for capturing that right mood, son," he'd claimed, handing me a weed to stick between my teeth. I'd noticed he'd torn it from some poison sumac, so I declined his offer, but neglected to inform him of his soon-to-be-discovered mistake.

He had Mom convinced that we'd all be on the cover of *Mountain Lifetimes Magazine* by Christmas before he was done. She was more excited than any of us. His "when I get paid, y'all get paid" pitch had worked like a charm. "Oh, take all the photos you want," Mom told him. "Have dinner with us. How about breakfast?" "A snack?" "Use the bathroom anytime you need." Dad didn't like that one.

But Christmas came and went. Then New Years. Valentine's Day. Easter. Mom's birthday. Spring was coming on and we hadn't heard from the guy.

Dad figured he owed us, not counting the pictures, about a hundred dollars in food alone. He had a big appetite for such a little guy. I think I could have beat him when we had our biscuits and gravy eating contest on the second morning, but he'd already been up taking pictures and building up an appetite and I'd slept in and was only watching cartoons. We didn't open the shop until eleven on Saturday mornings. That man could eat.

Fed up with Mom being so upset, Dad ended up calling *Mountain Lifetimes Magazine*, Inc., in Nashville over the whole thing, though Mom swore it might jinx our chances if we got on the wrong side of the magazine execs. Come to find out, they didn't know a Johnny G. Porter. Never had him on their payroll. Never heard of his "famous" mountain photography.

We got busy with some investigating of our own. It didn't take long to run him down. Come to find out he wasn't the real photographer in the family after all. He was a photographer's assistant to his wife who owned and ran Sassandra's Photography and Frame Shoppe, with help from their two teenagers, Brad and Todd. From their website it appeared most of their business was from wedding planning jobs and Confederate reenactment family packages. A family photo on a sunset or sunrise beach with everyone dressed in all white graced the top of the website. Dad said that was odd since the family was known for taking photos and wondered if they'd gotten a stranger on the beach to snap that shot.

When Uncle Archie, Dad, and I walked in to the lobby of their home and asked for a Union family photograph, Todd, the youngest of the two boys, was a little flustered. "I'm not sure where we keep all that gear. Let me get my step-dad," he told us, looking confused.

When Johnny G. appeared from behind the scenes, he had an apron on and a name tag. We all just smiled like he was expecting us. His eyes got as big around as a shrunken apple doll head. I thought he might run, but he froze.

"Todd, hey, um, I got this one. Why don't you go help your mother."

Todd huffed and walked out into the back.

"Howdy, Johnny," Dad said. Uncle Archie only nodded and grunted. I kept my mouth shut. "We're so glad to run into you. My wife's been awfully excited about that photo essay you were so hot and heavy to get. How's that turning out for ya? It's been a while."

He stuttered for a moment. "Well, *Mountain Lifetimes* decided to go in another direction, so . . ."

"Hmmph. That's awfully strange," Dad interrupted. "They told us they didn't know who the hell you were."

"They didn't say hell," Uncle Archie added, not bothering to look up from paging through the catalogue of studio products on the counter. "True. I added that part just now," Dad admitted. I was still keeping my mouth shut. That's when I learned the most Uncle Archie was convinced.

The poor man was a nervous wreck, in general it seemed, and long before ever running into us. Come to find out, his time with us had been during a fight with his business-owning wife. He'd struck out to make his way and prove himself as a standalone country photographer. We were going to be his best work. He was so sure of it was why he made all of those promises.

We never did tell Mom exactly where we went that weekend, but she thought the Civil War photo package we got at "what was that little spot called again" was real nice. She couldn't believe our luck, just happening in during their contest and winning the tenth-anniversary special giveaway: a one hour sitting with the master photographer herself, Sassandra "what was her last name again." We found a great place to display all those shots, too, right by the little door into the Underground Reunion.

The Art of Grief

This infamous strip of Route 17 wasn't quite a ninety-degree crook in the road, but it might as well have been at a certain point-of-no-return-speed which, according to the sheriff's deputy handling Dan's daughter's fatal accident, was at least fifty-five miles an hour. Given the impact's violence into the rock wall and lack of skidding, the car was probably traveling closer to seventy.

Those details should have mattered less to Dan by now, six months after the crash, but there he was, out along the highway, again, pacing the shoulder, eyeing the stretch of road up and down, up again, unsatisfied with the deputy's conclusions, the coroner's report. Crazed by the rumors. He'd even argued with eye-witnesses.

His daughter, Kate—their Katie—had only tapped her breaks for an instant, a man driving behind her reported. But how could that be? He'd been with her plenty of times driving through here, day or night. She was an excellent driver. An excellent kid.

But it was dark, Dan felt it was his responsibility to argue. Close to midnight. That boy was with her. The one she'd swore to marry soon. The one he'd swore she wouldn't. The one his wife, Julia, was warming up to. Surely that little fucker without a care of his own was a distraction: talking constantly, pawing at her, just being himself. Just being Jake. A punk.

Why else would his only daughter drive straight into the rock face of a mountainside?

At least the impact took their lives before the fireball ignited. Supposedly. Didn't it? But what sort of consolation is that? How was that supposed to make Julia and him feel better?

Dan gazed up the scorched stone by what little sun remained of the day, the formation of rock wall jutting up more than thirty feet before cedars grew magically rooted out of the dirtless topmost stones.

Right here, he thought.

He stood just where they'd hit, the white Mazda MX-3 they'd given her slightly airborne from ramping the shoulder ditch.

Here, yea high. The driver's front fender first.

The very spot his baby's spirit fled her body. Left the world. Left him and her mother in their corners, squared off, guilty and miserable. Lost. He was beyond the sobbing now. Past much anger. He'd been here at the spot too many times for all that.

When he stood here he couldn't help but remember the time they'd stood at the end of the pier at Kure Beach, North Carolina. Katie had released her birthday balloon, a pink number nine lifting and catching the shore breeze against a cloudless blue, all of them watching it shrink and shrink to a small round thing until it vanished. Katie had been too amazed by the strange beauty of the sight to tear up. They'd suspected she'd let go on purpose. When he stood here he wondered how a spirit dissipates. Out? Like a snap, gone in place? In all directions? Or a meandering, like a balloon on wind? Did it leave at all?

In the gravel and scrub weeds below the rock rested makeshift memorials from past accidents, the spot for his daughter's obviously most recent, but beginning to show signs of wear. There were wooden crosses, white paint flaking down to rawness. The red or white bows of sunlight-faded ribbon. The fake flowers turning lighter. Any real flowers, now brittle like dead autumn leaves. Some had photos thumbtacked or glued here and there. Even those photos faded in the sun and weather.

Katie's accident was the third at this spot. Four people had died there and another two nearly. One memorial had yellow night-road reflectors lining the cross, some attempt at preventing someone else from losing a child, going through that misery. Every little bit helped in a place seemingly designed for bad luck. Yet here stood Dan, wondering what really happened. What sort of luck had run out for their Katie?

Dan had her memorial flowers centered at the base of the wall of rock. He'd chosen a wreath of white carnations held tall with a metal tripod, positioned as near the spot she died as possible. A yellow sash crossed the middle reading *Daughter* in blue pretty, glittered cursive. Once the live flowers died, Dan made sure to replace them with an even larger wreath of white silk flowers, transferring the ribbon. Family and Katie's friends and others accumulated contributions around the foot of the wreath, turning it shrine-like and beautiful for a time. Now the ground was a mix of barely recognizable faded flowers, rain-ruined stuffed animals, slushy handmade cards, and black-and-gold pompoms from her old cheer-team friends from high school. Dan pulled the single white carnation he'd bring on every visit and pushed the stem into what was left of the wreath. It was a stark newness to the ruination.

On this visit he noticed something new on the rock facing. Rather than new spray-painted graffiti, someone had scrubbed away a portion of sooty blackness from the burned rock, writing out *We Miss U*.

He spat on his finger and plied the tip forcefully down along a portion of smooth stone, fully aware of his morbid act, of his daughter's DNA surely combined in the ashy substance he was pulling away. What he'd scrubbed left a lighter line. As a painter he was immediately aware of how a solvent, like turpentine, would more easily pull the crusty soot away. It set him to thinking.

He'd set up the accident site memorial mostly after being so disappointed with Katie's mundane gravesite. Dan's wife's family had bought everyone plots in Memory Rose Gardens, a for-profit, flat stone only, easy to mow, boring-as-shit industrial graveyard business, started by a townie with a little money and some semiflat land on their hands. Katie's grave was lost among all the others. He'd longed to bury her with a big tall stone that reflected her personality—loud and energetic. Maybe one of those aboveground chambers like down in a New Orleans cemetery, covered with carvings of angels and crosses. The more extravagant the better. But that didn't fly here in the mountains. That was too flamboyant. Too Catholic in a town without enough Catholics to warrant even a Catholic church.

Her roadside memorial, bigger than the rest he'd made sure, was still hard to see at a glance, especially passing in a car along that dangerous curve. Katie deserved something better. Something remarkable. Of course, Dan was prone to obsessions and grandiosity. He knew it. His wife Julia knew it. Even Katie would joke about it. But if something was worth obsessing over, this was surely it.

The next Saturday Dan was at the spot again with all the materials he'd need to make Katie proud. Extension ladder, work rags, bottles of turpentine, jugs of water, a bucket of various-sized brushes.

He'd lied to Julia. Told her he was at the school studio working on a new project, something that would take some weeks to finish. He'd be gone more than usual. Truth be told, both were fine with the added time apart. When Dan spent time on his art it was proof his dream of breaking from his tiny bubble of work wasn't quite dead. Julia was glad to have more time to brood over whatever it was this week she was regretting about still being with Dan. At least that's how it felt to Dan since the accident. It was as if Katie's existence, in living, had dammed up what was building over the years. When the dam broke, her death, anything seemed fair game. Resentment. Guilt. Cruelty. Up went a taller, thicker wall.

A week of research had amassed too many ideas to pick from. There were endless images of memorials, even project collections of memorial sites. Research on the frequency of roadside memorials throughout the country. It was a growing phenomenon.

In the midst of digesting all that material, he wondered what image, what likeness might offer an air of consolation at this spot that was otherwise a heartbreaking place of gloom for so many families. Something iconic, recognizable. A paradox, offering love in a place of pain.

On one of many sleepless nights, while Dan roamed the house wearing himself down chasing some variance of fatigue, he ended up in Katie's room. He didn't often go there, though his wife tended to. She kept it just as it had been—her personal shrine. As if she was away at camp and coming back the next morning, back to the breakfast table, all excited for a new school year.

Music posters on the walls. A senior year book on the dresser. Boxes of jewelry. Closet of perfectly aligned clothes. Colorful throw pillows all over. A stained-glass chime rocking in the window lit by weak streetlight.

Her rosary was on the bedstand, along with a little brass crucifix she'd picked up at the flea market. They were Catholic, but he wondered if Katie adhered to any true sacred use of these objects. Or were they just curiously pretty? He hoped the former. She had a way about her, a forgiving ease he'd called angelic when she was much younger. As she'd grown up that ease had manifested into a demeanor making it easy for people to open up to her. She complained how kids at school confided too much to her. It made her uncomfortable. Dan wondered what secrets she'd taken to her grave.

The next day, he returned to the roadside with a vision. He was going to take this damned soot holding captive his daughter's death and turn it into a crucifix as large as the burnt section of flat rock would allow. It was at least twenty feet high and fifteen feet wide at the best places. He would use turpentine-soaked rags to remove the soot down to the lighter, clean and pure rock, creating a giant image of Christ on the cross. This would be the ultimate roadside memorial. His greatest work of art. Maybe Julia would even be proud of it.

Dan envisioned a slight outcropping of stone, up at just the right height, as the face of Jesus. It would offer a 3D effect, at the right size. All else would exude from this malformed portion of what was otherwise a near perfect canvas.

He raised the extension ladder, placing himself face-to-face with the plain stone outcropping, lifting the rope that brought up the bucket of brushes, rags, and turpentine. He'd attempted no sketches. No notes. He trusted his mind and hands, the will of the rock, his emotional state, to work out the plan. To find a harmony, if one was to be found.

What wasn't there, and he knew it all too well, was a complete faith. Enough, at least. Some, yes. He approached the task like any other art installation, like a project, not as prayer. He just wasn't there yet. He didn't know what to expect at the top of the ladder. It felt only like work. Determined work, yes. But not the freeing gift he probably had fantasized would come. Still, he began.

For two hours he worked without coming down, at first, working the solvents softly over the soot. Ruining a rag quickly. Then another. Having to scrub harder in places. Chip off harder pieces.

Learning where and how to apply force to make the darkness vanish with the cleaning. The metaphor wasn't lost on him; this cleaning away of the past, he thought. This negative replacing of a good thing over horror. Calling forth the image. A little steel brush. Smoothing with the rag. A gradual finding how many colors existed down through the soot. The differing shades of stone.

And behold: the face of Christ emerged from the stubborn rock. Affirmation to Dan that God might be in the work after all. In a place of loss. Of hatred of loss. Roughened face. The facial bones, sunken cheeks, some semblance of a beard. The struggling visage. Eye to eye emerging.

He stared at the personality suddenly there. Was there pain in the face? Pity? Compliance with destiny? Miraculous fate.

He worked the crown of thorns away from the soot with deeply rubbed streaks, learning more as he went, letting a few heavy dabs of turpentine streak down like caustic blood, added a long exaggerated neck weighted by a convincingly tired head, working this into the naked taut chest and torso, the body appearing stretched and pained, then to the distressed waist, pulling away the flesh tones in broad strokes with the rags and large brushes, ribs nearly exposed through stressed flesh, so that by sundown the image was a limbless torso, thin, tallish. Recognizable.

Yes. Recognition.

Julia had long given up trying to keep him from going back out to *that rotten place*, she'd call it, among other names. That hurt. Didn't she have a shrine of sorts in Katie's bedroom, plus the bland cemetery she visited as much as she pleased? As far as Dan was concerned, the spot on the roadside was Katie's truest resting place, not some homogenized rectangle in Memory Rose Gardens.

He didn't worry about Julia seeing him out here. She went out of her way to avoid the accident area and had never contributed any thought to the memorial. She despised it. How different they were as people. The stress of their daughter's death only drove a larger wedge through the middle of their already precarious marriage.

Life would occasionally flow into what resembled normal for a day or two, the anger subsiding, the blame fading. But the simplest of agitations would set them off. A dinner out, ruined when one of them was triggered by an empty chair. Where to put that grief, but against someone you love who might keep taking it?

You let her run wild. No wonder she was out that late.

You never wanted her to grow up. No wonder she rebelled.

By the next weekend Dan was back, this time working on Christ's midsection wrapped in abstract cloth, the limbs elongated and exaggerated, weak legs bent slight at the knees.

He caught himself talking out loud. Mumbling as he worked.

"I think I know a little of how you feel. So tired. Right on the verge of giving up." Dan knew how ridiculous a statement that was. How could he know even a fraction of the Lord's discomfort at the end? The passion?

If he thought too long on the state of life, there was plenty to give up on. Their marriage. Julia believing in him. His bothering to do anything but teach, rather than his own art. On faith in anything, really. How easy it would be to just float in apathy. He worked the region around the wound into the side, through the ribs, where the Roman guard stabbed upward with the spear.

Then the mangled feet. He worked on these without the ladder, exaggerating, too, a spike through them and into the cross's wood he'd fashioned behind the aspect of ruined flesh, bringing down the effect of wood into a drawn pile of rocks where the cross appeared to be held sturdily. His own version of the Place of the Skulls. Golgotha. A hill where thousands died. Tens of thousands. Countless men, women. Children.

As he labored the burnt surface he felt more and more meditative, as if the prayer was coming. Perhaps he was needing to see the whole body up there, completed. The more he concentrated on the details now, the less he dwelled on the underlying morbidness of the act. He would forget, for a blessed time that his daughter's last instance of breath was here in this slurry coating his hands and streaming down his filthy arms, off his elbows. Covering his shirt and pants. Splattering his face. The taste staying with him. In the mix of scents he picked up from the work. From the mud he created at the rock base from stomping in water, soot, and pooled cleaning spirits.

But then he'd need to see about the composition and step back to look, nearly into the road, and the realization of what he was doing would hit him, as if a vehicle had blindly sideswiped him. A vision, like a movie, of what must have happened would play and replay, right there where he stood, the sound of the engine, the tires into the shoulder area, the gravel and ditch. The stone. If he let it, as he was taking in the wholeness of the piece, catching the eyes up there gazing down at the imagined explosion, it would overwhelm him and he'd almost give up on the day. But the releasing prayer would come back and settle the aching: *Just let a little of the pain go away.* Then it was back to work.

Someone in a car would pull up and park. No one usually disturbed him. They'd watch for a little while, curious, or were only monitoring his progress since last time they passed by. Some would slow down in the curve and snap a picture. Some might yell out, but he was never paying attention enough to really hear.

The arms were outstretched taut, uncomfortable. Wrists spiked through just like the feet by long exaggerated nails. It was hard getting the 3D effect of the spikes. He made the top bar of wood not much thicker than Christ's arms, envisioning an emphasis on the dying body's pull of hanging weight, earth pulling, the heaviness of the head barely held up now, appearing to lean forward and to the side. Above the head, a tall extension of the main supporting pole.

It was finished.

He dropped the ladder out of the way. Moved the buckets of tools aside. Stood back to take it all in. The wholeness.

Was it? Finished?

Something was wrong. An artist knows this, when a thing isn't quite right. The face. Something about the face.

The 3D effect of that section of rock wasn't cooperating. The right cheek protruded too much. The head leaned, as if Christ was about to give up, the face nearly fallen, death taking him. A perfect effect. But that one imperfect cheek. Dan stepped closer. To the side. Yes, too much rock at that spot. The face was to be as real as possible. The anguish clear from the road.

He looked in his trunk. No hammer. No chisel. Nothing that would work in the floorboard of the truck. No harder rock that might do the job. So he went home.

Dreams flooded his sleep in the night.

The face up on the rock was moved. He stood below, at the foot of this cross of oddity. The eyes shifted down, staring, neither judging nor neutral. Christ's dying eyes simply were. The right corner of the mouth raised with a half grimace, accentuating the right cheek, lifting it, pushing it out of place and tightening the skin. The skin there split and water and blood rushed forth, the eyes straining wild at the developed wound as it spread, letting out a faster rivering of pinkish life fluids. The eyes closed. The head fell heavy to the chest.

He didn't bother telling Julia about the dreams. She never told him what made her wail in her sleep. Why would he share this gift of strangeness? He assumed it was a gift.

Dan was up on the ladder again the next afternoon, this time with a hammer and chisel. That one chunk of stone had been a thorn in his dreams. He started with light taps, fearing the whole face would fall away with too hard a smack.

Nothing budged. Only tiny flecks and sparks resulted from the first few strikes. He tempered his force. Worked harder along a natural crack that hinted might be weak enough to give way, getting up under the smallest of holes to gain leverage. He struck the spot again, only slightly harder. Then again. A little more. Too much would ruin everything, wouldn't it?

Something snapped with a low bass of a pop. It resonated through the chisel, down through the ladder into his feet, the shock like an echoing pulse plunging away from him into the hill. Sudden, then absorbed. A piece of rock half the size of his fist fell into his palm.

He froze, fearing what he'd done.

The broken portion was wet on the underside.

Dan smelled the water first, its essence cool and fresh on his face. Then the soft stream bled from under the right eye where the rock had fallen away. He blinked. The face was done.

By the time he'd climbed down and lowered the ladder, a gentle line of water ran from the eye and cheek, glistening down the rock as if falling through the air from Christ's face, until it dripped from a spot just ledged enough for the stream to drip fast on its own into true air. It was creating the tiniest of waterfalls at waist level. Dan stood wondering what he was watching. Witnessing. It ran black with muck. He had to resist the urge to run his fingers under the drips.

He was quietly stunned, still in the moment, taking in what was surely a miracle.

A miracle of what he couldn't say. All he saw was the crying Christ, rendered by him on this rock of death. What it meant, or not, was beyond his doing. Beyond any understanding.

If that hadn't happened, he'd have probably stuck around, admired the work. Been satisfied. But it didn't belong to him now, did it? This sudden flowing water changed things. If he'd needed something tangible to signal the work was finished, this was it. Finished for Katie, yes. But maybe for something bigger than even this pain and confusion and frustration.

He had to leave. Something told him it was time to go now. For a while. Or was he just scared?

Let the water do its work. Go away and let the water find the fire.

He knew he'd spend the drive home trying to explain away what he'd witnessed. But he'd fail in the end.

Still feeling in shock, he slowly collected his bucket of tools and carried them along with his ladder to the truck, packed it all away for the last time, strapped down the ladder and pulled into the curve of the road.

A few days later Julia was at the kitchen table. She was waiting for him to get home from work. It was late Thursday afternoon. She never did this, sitting and waiting, doing nothing.

"What's up, honey?"

"The sheriff called, Dan."

He didn't respond.

"About some traffic jam you've created out on 17." She said it like a question, as if he'd know exactly what she was talking about.

Not a sound.

"Is that what you've been doing, your project, when you said you were at the studio? You were out there painting rocks, or whatever Donny was trying to explain on the phone."

What could Dan say? He sat.

"People are parking along the road. Lined up, leaving shit at that, that, memorial spot as you like to call it, causing traffic hazards. What if someone wrecks? They died, too?"

He stood abruptly.

"Watch your mouth, Julia. You wouldn't stand for me talking like that about Katie's grave, would you?" His anger filled the room. "I've created something good there. Something amazing's happened. If you'd only . . ."

His wife was up, already walking from the kitchen, done with the conversation. He'd have left her for good right then if he hadn't been so damn tired.

" . . . if you'd only go see . . ."

It took another day, but he finally forced himself to go out there. This idea had grown larger than him. It was more than art. More than his art, wasn't it? It was becoming its own entity. That was frightening, for some proof to have answered the work. Without his being there to over watch it. Whatever was happening wasn't his any longer.

Julia was right. Parked cars lined the road. A few people were making their way up the shoulder on foot. Some carried empty jars. Others returned with filled containers. Orange cones blocked off the right lane. Ahead, a deputy was making sure traffic merged out of the far-right lane away from cars pulling back in traffic. He looked some bothered.

Half a dozen people congregated at the base of the rock.

What is happening here?

Already the other memorial spots had grown with new trinkets and colors. There was a shimmer of candle light among the people, around their hands and faces, at their feet.

Dan carefully mixed into the crowd, listening, watching.

The falling water line down from Christ's face was cleaned clear now, along the stones, the stream about an inch across at its widest. A steady little river ran off the ledge and someone had placed a clay bowl under it. It was full and shimmering, surrounded by lit white candles. A foot-tall white porcelain statue of the Virgin sat on a nearby rock. She was praying. The wax from candles dripped down and off onto the gravely mud. A man dipped his hand into where the water splashed the soot at their feet, stood, reached over with his hand and made the sign of the cross on a woman's forehead. She hugged the man with a smile and walked away with a mason jar of sparkling water she'd filled from the little waterfall.

It was an amazing site, but something about the candle flames nearly set him off. It was the fire. The flames. Here. Katie. What the hell were they doing? What had he done, inviting all this? This wasn't what he wanted at all. Hadn't he envisioned a quiet, contemplative spot? Or, what had he wanted? A piece of art to be untouched on the side of the road, admired from a distance?

Or touched, intimately, like a true shrine?

Just like this. By all these people.

He noticed a familiar someone. She was standing by a little girl who was kneeling on a cushion and facing the rock wall. She was a teacher from the local Catholic school.

The woman recognized Dan and stepped to him.

"You have done something wonderful here, Mr. Williams. May God bless you for it."

What could he say?

"I was only trying to remember my daughter better, Rita."

"My daughter, Maria, insisted on stopping this week. It scared her at first, when the headlights hit the image and the sun was going down. But then she wanted to stop and pray. She said, *Jesus is crying, Momma*. Maria placed her hands under the stream and filled them and splashed the water on her own face. She said, *These are his own tears.* She swore it. That night she dreamed about your daughter, Mr. Williams. She described her like she knew her, that Kate was here standing by the fountain telling a long line of people how this water would help them."

Dan looked at the little girl, kneeled nearby with a rosary hanging from her clasped hands, her lips moving quietly.

"How old is she?"

"She's only seven, Mr. Williams. She talked about it at school before I could stop her."

He looked around. A woman was setting another statue of the Virgin nearby, this one by Kate's wreath, the ground area becoming more and more crowded with offerings.

"How can she say that? How can she possibly—"

"She has no reason to lie, sir."

A man about Dan's age was arranging new flowers around another memorial. Up to now it had been neglected, but now it was enlivened with fresh flowers and a framed photo of a pretty woman in a red dress.

Dan walked over.

"I'd all but forgotten about setting this up for her," the man confessed. "She's been gone for seven years already."

His name was Allen. His wife, Sue, had died here. Hit by another car.

"I kept up the spot for a few years. Came out every few weeks. I felt closer to her here than at her grave, you know?"

"I know what you mean," Dan agreed, laying a hand on the man's shoulder.

"But somewhere along the way I lost track. I feel terrible about that."

Dan nodded.

"But I dreamed about her a few days ago. I swear to God. She came to me. She was standing in a river. Water up to her knees. She was smiling in the sun. I had to come back out here. I found all this was going on."

An aging woman noticed Dan. Approached holding her rosary in a tight-fisted grip.

"Bless me, Mr. Williams. For your daughter's sake."

It was Betty Jenkins who ran the cupcake shop downtown. They'd known each other for years. He'd taken Katie to her shop for treats when she was a little girl.

He backed away a step, wondering on the strange favor.

"What do you want me to do, Betty?" Really, what could he do? *Hadn't he done enough now?*

"Make the sign of the cross on me, please. For Kate's sake. We'll always remember her."

The old woman grinned, appearing happy. For her, the spot wasn't morbid in the least. People weren't making much noise. They were whispering excitedly. Gathering some of the water and leaving with it. Bathing their faces with their palms. Dipping their fingers and making the sign of the cross. Cupping their hands under the water, letting it gather, and sipping it.

Jesus, he whispered. Was that safe?

But wasn't this exactly what he wanted? Katie remembered in some incredible way. Some miraculous way. Here was the chance, now, the tangible gift.

"You of all people should do this, Dan." Betty held his hand in both of hers, embracing it with a warmth that surprised him.

He leaned over between two people gazing up at his work, work no longer his, now claimed by others. A slight spray, catching gold flashes of late afternoon light, fell on everyone's faces. Dan stretched his arm to the rock and plied his thumb down a dampened portion of the stone and brought it back. It was streaked with the oily sootiness that was ever the reminder of his daughter's lost being, there in a last tangible sense, yet expressed around him now by these visitors. In the mystery of their curiosity. Their faith in something growing here. Down the highway people were still parking and coming up the road.

"Thank you, Katie," he whispered, turning to the waiting woman. People stood back.

He pressed his darkened thumb to her forehead, closing his own eyes, then softly dragged it downward in one motion.

"I bless you, Betty," he said very quietly.

Then from left to right, completing the cross.

" . . . in the name of Saint Katherine of the Fiery Rock . . ."

Benny and the Hill's Angels

Benny didn't mind walking his paper route. He could take his bike when he wanted to, if the tires were up and the chain didn't go cockeyed and the seat wasn't falling off. Walking was a lot nicer, he thought, up the hill a bit where the sun reached for a stretch, then down where it disappeared as the trees seemed like they stole the sun away for a half mile. He liked the warmth starting him off, how it cooled as he eased into the shadows down through the long hollow where the blacktop turned to gravel and then to dirt by the end of the road at the Thompson Cemetery.

Delivering *The Labor County Times* wasn't that bad. He'd had worse jobs. Like last year during tax season when he'd had to dress up like "Lady Liberty" for Bill Sampson's Tax Service and Tanning Salon. It sounded like a lot of fun at first. Almost no one had recognized him as he marched the sidewalk, performing his required patriotic military-style salute of passing drivers. He'd salute people walking by on the sidewalk, too, not because he had to, but because he liked it.

The costume was troublesome, though. The spiked headdress was heavy on his head and his wrinkled turquoise gown was always snagging under his size-fourteen tennis shoes as he tried juggling the big red arrow sign that read TAXES on one side and TANS on the other. He'd toss it up with a flip and catch it. Spin it. Shake it around real good. But the wind would grab hold of it occasionally and he'd chase it down in traffic, tripping over his gown, the headdress leaning crooked, covering his eyes. He'd be avoiding looking people in the eyes as they screeched to a halt to avoid this goofy Goliath of an animated Statue of Liberty tearing into the intersection about to cause a pile-up. The sign ended up with at least three streaks of tire marks on it. Two on the TAXES side and one on the TANS side.

The hardest thing for Benny was keeping the arrow pointing in the right direction. Now that wasn't easy at all.

"Quit pointin' across the road to that other tax place, Benny!" Mr. Sampson, the boss, would holler while working inside with a customer.

When Mr. Sampson wanted Benny to get his face "tan-painted," as he called it, since that was one of their "value-added" service marketing strategies, Benny was having nothing of it. He quit and went back to his paper route.

It was when some of the kids along Seeping Hollow Road yelled mean things at him, though, that he was pretty close to quitting this job again. Quit and start thumpin' on someone. He hadn't done that in a long time. Once or twice was enough for word to get around. Now they'd just call out from behind fastened doors and wide trees.

"Frankenbenny . . . Oh, Frankenbenny!" they'd hoot, trying to rile him.

"Chickens," he'd whisper under his breath.

"How's the paper route Big Ol' Benny Boy?"

"Cowardly chickens . . ." he'd hiss a little louder as his pace quickened.

Aunt Lee's voice was always cheerleading in his head.

"Don't you ever show you're scared, Benny. Not even if you're shaking in them size-fourteen shoes. No matter what or when, don't look scared."

But Aunt Lee had it all wrong, he figured. He wasn't really scared when things like this happened. It was more like he got nervous. More and more nervous the more people aggravated him. It made something inside him feel bad. He could never really explain it to his aunt.

"Cowardly chicken livers!" he'd finally scream up the road, teeth grinding, fists balled, an undammable emotion welling up. He'd want to break something. Anything. Then the shower of half-rotten walnuts would come raining down like an angry storm of staining black hail from behind houses and up behind the tree line's safe thickness. He'd never flinch. Just like Aunt Lee taught him. And if anyone ever thought they'd get within an arm's reach of him? Well, that just never happened, now did it? There probably wasn't a boy his age or older, or man for that matter, in the whole county, that wouldn't think twice before running crossed ways with Benny.

Some claimed Benny was the largest seventeen-year-old ever to live in Labor County. Those same people figured he'd probably have the record for eighteen too when the time came. His overstuffed canvas paper harness was tiny on his six-foot-five-inch frame as he'd trot along, fishing out tight rolled papers and seeing if he could slice one through a meaner family's screen door.

"Remember, mean offspring's a sign of mean parenting skills," Aunt Lee always said. She was always giving Benny one-liner advice.

And he could hit about anything. Tossing a rolled paper wasn't any different than a good-sized hard granny apple. One time, when Axel Fieldmore, of the Seeping Hollow Fieldmores, flung a gravel at him from up on the hill, he saw it coming and deflected it with his paper bag like it was a shield and just kept on smiling, taking easy aim and leisurely flinging his attacker's mother's paper into their algae filled birdbath sitting in the front yard's lake of mud.

Try readin' that one, Feeeeld-more.

The image of a paper sailing from his hand, arc-less, splitting a screen and landing all the way back in their kitchen made him giggle. And he knew where the kitchens were, too, since most all of these old mine shacks were built the same. Front porch, living room, hall with a bedroom on each side, a bathroom, and the kitchen way in the back before the back porch. It was like some monster cookie cutter had swooped through back in the thirties and plopped them down in little neat rows on the way to the now abandoned mine entrances. He liked their different colors, like dusty Easter eggs.

Where his own kitchen was, on the other hand, back at his Aunt Lee's, was a little different story. Sometimes he teased he couldn't find it. "Aunt Lee! Where'd you move the kitchen to?"

It never quite looked like a kitchen, all stuffed and stacked with unkitcheny things. His aunt was a terrible "whorder" his cousin, Jenkins, once told him. He'd even spelled it out for him.

In fact, he'd walked into the wrong house once, not realizing it wasn't Aunt Lee's, until he noticed he could see the floor and furniture and then heard Mrs. Foley, obviously not his aunt, scream and hop up from her taped soaps with Benny just standing there confused as to whether everyone sat watching soaps at four in afternoon in so little clothes. She'd cancelled her subscription to *The Labor County Times* the very next day. No explanation to his boss. Maybe that was her way of saving his job, though he remembered her hollering threats of reporting him as she chased him out of the house throwing old outdated *TV Monthly* magazines at him.

He'd just started his route and was making his way on the down side of the first hill when he noticed two legs and an arm sticking awkwardly out of a ditch off the road. He'd almost missed it, but what grabbed his attention was the blinding sunshine glancing off the chrome wheels of some of the fanciest roller skates he'd ever seen up close. Then there was the scratched and bleeding pretty calves they were strapped to along with the limp hand at the end of a bent arm with blood running from the elbow. He tip-toed up and leaned over so he could see the rest of the body. Yep, it was a girl. He'd figured so since the legs looked so smooth and there was shiny black polish on the fingernails.

He thought for a pretty long minute, staring down the girl's limp form and wondering what to do. Aunt Lee always said to give things a lot of thought so he wouldn't jump off a cliff if someone else did. He noticed her red helmet with a long fluffy golden wing hand-painted across the side. Should he leave her alone? Get help? He couldn't just leave her, could he? And who was it? And what would Aunt Lee do?

Benny was a mess of nerves and not a little lightheaded suddenly. He righted himself and paced a few steps, looking at her again, but shaking his head and diverting his eyes, a pang of confusing guilt hitting him for spying her just lying there, maybe dead, maybe alive. Something told him she was awfully pretty. That helmet sure was. He stared at the painted gold wing. There was a white glowing halo painted around the helmet, like the one round the Lord's head on that velvet painting hanging over the couch back home, the one of Jesus walking on the water. The one with the other man sinking and reaching for him.

What in the world—*or not of this world*—had he found?

A painful moan floated up from the weeds. Benny hopped back. The crooked arm moved. She wasn't dead.

Grabbing an ankle, he dragged the body up into the road as carefully as he could, fully expecting to bear witness to the miracle of white wings resting down her back as her body cleared the tangle of kudzu and wild sunflowers.

But there were none. Just a pair of gold airbrushed wings stretching from her shoulder blades to her waist, the sort of painting like people got at the mall on license plates for Christmas. Then there was the answer. Above the wings was her name in gold boldness across the shoulders, the answer to who, *or what*, she was. *Angel*.

His jaw dropped open with the possibility of it. What if this was an angel?

An angel named Angel?

And God had hurled her down to earth just for him to find and save. Didn't Aunt Lee talk about God sending people angels in their times of need? He didn't feel particularly in need at the moment, but he figured God knew best.

Maybe it was a test. He hated tests. Maybe hard times were coming. He craned his head up carefully and checked the darkening sky, wondering if any more angelic bodies might be on the way. Or maybe a storm.

Benny stretched her out and turned her over. Her body was ragdoll light. She stirred and he got down on his knees and leaned in a bit closer. Her breath smelled of strawberry gum. "Hill's Angels" was airbrushed in black across the front of her helmet. The mystery deepened.

She looked asleep.

"Are you okay?" he whispered, almost to quietly for him to even hear.

No response.

"Are you okay?" A little louder.

Did she even speak the same if she wasn't from here?

He studied the dark makeup around her eyelids, an earring through black lipsticked lips, a purple streak thinning down sweat-tangled hair and out of the helmet. Dark, crow black, pretty hair. He didn't know her. But she sure was pretty. He was sure he knew everyone in town. At least everyone knew him it seemed. A break of thunder cracked up over the hill across town. Maybe she was an angel, and this was a disguise. A tricky test, he figured, giggling at God's sense of humor, which Aunt Lee always pointed out to him when things in life turned funny.

Was this like those crazy tests at school? The ones he wasn't any good at that ended up holding him back. The "only Benny left behind" tests, Aunt Lee called them. Too many choices. He'd always felt like drawing a huge circle over the entire test page. Putting eyes and a smiling mouth in the middle.

All the answers seemed right. Go get help from one of the houses close by. Use their phone to call an ambulance. The police. Leave her alone right here and mind your own business. Run back to the house for Aunt Lee and come back. Finish his paper route. He finally decided to take her home and figure it out then.

His voice was calm as he lifted her limp form and hoisted her effortlessly over the shoulder opposite the paper harness.

"It's gonna be alright now," he assured her, carefully patting along what he imagined was real wings down her back. "We'll get Aunt Lee to help . . . she'll know what to do. She always knows just what to do. You'll like her."

It was a half mile back home, and though the girl wasn't too heavy to start with, Benny was pretty winded by the time he rounded Breakman's Corner and came eye to eye with Mrs. Matthews standing there on her porch getting ready to scan the obituaries. And, of course, it just so happened she was the one customer warning him regular about never getting caught down in the holler near the cemetery after dark. She was the most superstitious woman around, according to Aunt Lee. So here Benny came carting off what looked like a dirtied and bloodied up dead body out of the holler as fast as his legs could still churn. Mrs. Matthews was on her cordless phone talking a mile a minute before he even passed her mailbox. Something about that big Lee kid that broke her window last year with the paper and wondering what sort of devilishness he'd pulled out of the cemetery and was taking home to that crazy gossip of an aunt.

By the time he got to his aunt's driveway and across the yard and up on the porch and through the small foot route that was cleared through the living room and to the magazine-stacked couch, Benny was huffing and puffing so loud that Aunt Lee had to get up from her afternoon nap to see what he'd gotten into, figuring he'd gotten chased by dogs again. But what was waiting for her heavy eyes, stretched out on the couch and done up in the biggest mess of roller-skating gear she'd ever seen, woke her up real fast. Benny was standing there all sheepish with that "I need your help" look, the one that just melted her heart every single time.

"Lord, Benny . . . what is that?"

"Aunt Lee . . . well, it's a girl."

"Ya think?" she hissed at him.

" . . . and, I think she's an angel," Benny spoke, looking down in a gaze of increasing admiration. He was pretty sure he'd fallen in love with the girl between passing Mrs. Matthew's place and the peak of the holler road, which he explained in detail to his aunt.

"Well, she is a pretty thing, I'll give you that much," she agreed. "Bit too much of that Elmo makeup," she added. Benny knew she meant Emo, but he didn't correct her.

"You think God sent her down here for some reason?"

She smirked with that "you box of rocks" look.

"What foolishness are you spoutin', boy? She ain't no real angel!"

Benny looked at his aunt, hurt like, then back at the groaning girl. "Well I think she is," he offered in earnest. He knelt.

"Are you gonna be okay?"

Aunt Lee kicked a gigantic tub of toilet paper and wet wipes to the side and made her way over to get a better look. The girl sighed in pain and cracked an eyelid open with a grimace, scanning the foreign room with the one eye, Benny's big black glasses and wide grin of both worry and eagerness greeting her focusing vision. A reddening pump knot was growing right between her eyes. She rubbed it with a wince.

"Hit your head when you fell, did ya?" Benny asked, sounding almost afraid of her.

She looked around, confused, overwhelmed by the state of the room. It looked like a chaotic warehouse, but then she realized it was just someone's home, a very well-stocked house of mostly unidentifiable cardboard boxes and Del-Mart bags and plastic containers.

"Naw . . ." she answered, trying to dismiss the pain. "I was doin' just fine till that damn june bug hit me. I never saw it comin'."

If there was a question in Benny's mind as to whether he was really in love or not, the sound of her voice finished the job. It was soft, just as he'd imagine an angel's might be, even if she had cussed. He bet Aunt Lee wouldn't wrestle a bar of soap into an angel's filthy mouth, would she?

Benny furled his brow in wonder. "A june bug hit you tween the eyes? And knocked you out?"

He let loose with what Angel could only assume was a laugh. She thought it was more like a muffled half stick of giggly dynamite trying to escape his mouth and nose. The tremor rolled through the house, reminding her of when the mines blew things up.

"Lord, don't get him started," Aunt Lee warned. "You've never seen a man his size giggle so hard."

"No. I don't think I blacked out till I hit the road and busted the back of my head." She rubbed the back of her skull through the helmet.

Benny finally calmed down. "Well, you sure are lucky you didn't hurt those skates . . . or that pretty helmet of yours." Benny stared at the words "Hill's Angels" again.

She gave him an odd look, gently touching the pump knot. "Yea. I'm lucky like that."

Benny gave his aunt a look like he wanted her to stop staring at his special guest.

"Well, younguns, you know what always makes things better, especially when you've wiped out skatin' on a gravel road and knocked yourself clean into a coma?"

Benny already knew the answer.

"Chocolate milk!" he yelled, startling the girl.

She was already headed into the kitchen, high-stepping over a fifty-pound bag of pinto beans and five-foot stack of unopened cat litter. That Benny could remember, they didn't own a cat and never had.

He lowered his voice, quite respectful like, and implied the question he was busting at the seams to ask.

"Your shirt says . . . Angel on it." He gave a little nod and a half wink, like she'd know exactly what he was getting at.

"Mhm. That's me."

She sat up slowly and pulled off the helmet, gawking at the state of the room. A living room ought to be livable, she thought. This one was just barely.

"I'm Benny. That's my aunt in there makin' us the chocolate milk. If she can find some. I know, this place needs some straightenin', but Aunt Lee says she knows exactly where everything's at."

A crash in the kitchen and some frustrated mumbles weren't very convincing.

He stuck his hand out to shake hers. It swallowed Angel's up.

"Where you from . . . Angel?" he asked, knowing the answer already, but trying to be polite.

She thought a moment. Her eyes felt like they were crossing from the headache. "Over on Hitch Street. You know it? About a mile from here?"

"I know it. I had one dang paper customer all the way out there once." He patted the paper satchel still hanging around his shoulder, proud like and smiled. "I've got my very own paper route."

She looked and nodded at the half-full bag.

"Looks like you've got some still to deliver."

"Well, I had to carry you back here, didn't I?"

"You carried me?"

"I did."

"All the way?"

"I did."

"By yourself?"

"I did."

"You done a lot."

Aunt Lee tripped back into the living room nearly spilling the extra-strength chocolate milks, with marshmallows, a reusable Big Slurp cup from Uncle Freeman's Quik Pick #2 for Benny and a regular tall glass for Angel. Benny held the door for Angel and they both went out to the screened front porch. It was suspiciously clean. *Ain't no reason for everyone to see what I got*, Aunt Lee would say, always insisting on a tidy front porch. *People talk enough as it is.*

They sat there, awkward in silence, Benny nervous and wondering about this mysterious girl, of whom he couldn't take eyes off, and Angel, feeling so embarrassed she could just die from the accident, but grateful this big lug was making over her so much. She hadn't had much attention lately.

"Thank you."

"Welcome."

Benny stared at the skates and to the helmet she was cradling in her scratched-up arms.

"You got a little grass stuck in your helmet there." She smiled, plucking the sour grass out of one of the helmet's vents.

"I've probably got grass stuck in places other than this." She nearly flew out of her skates and spilled her drink when Benny burst into one of the loudest string of giggles she'd ever heard. His body shook, and the more he tried to keep the giggles in, the more he giggled and the louder it got and the more chocolate milk streamed from the corner of his mouth. That it didn't stream from his nose, which had happened more than once, was a miracle he thought she might have something to do with. Then she cracked up, figuring it was about to fly out of his nose any second. They made the whole porch rattle and even the '88 Nascar chimes Aunt Lee bought from the flea market were jingling.

Eventually Benny couldn't take it anymore and finally asked what happened.

Angel gave a little smirk at the idea of explaining such an embarrassing ordeal. It seemed all of her big plans were falling apart.

"I was practicing my skating," she told him, lifting a bruised leg and tilting a skate. "I'm a Roller Derby girl."

"A say what?"

"Roller Derby. Don't you know what Roller Derby is?"

"No." He looked embarrassed.

"Oh, it's so much fun," she squealed, standing and taking a defensive position like she was ready to take a hit, forearm out front, knees bent, skates balanced, head low.

"You skate around in a circle and grab people's hands and whip them forward and the other team hip-and-shoulder checks you trying to knock you down and not let you pass. It can get real rough. I follow a bunch of teams all over the country. The Rat Town Rollers, the Big Town Roller Girls, the Richmond Roller Femmes. I love it!"

"Y'all skate around on a half-gravel road and try to knock each other out?" Benny asked, very confused by now.

"No, man," she sniped. "We skate on a flat place, like a basketball court or something. It's called flat track. You can fall down pretty hard, but the old days of knockin' each other out are pretty much over." She looked disappointed.

Benny tried to follow.

"I was practicin' out on the road. Sometimes I just skate and skate and skate. I end up out in the middle of nowhere I get so distracted, like my mind drifts off. My team's name is The Hill's Angels, cause my last name's Hill and all. Get it?"

Benny thought that was funny. But her little disguise didn't fool him one bit. He'd play along. Then he wondered, what if she'd just forgotten who she really was? She'd hit her head, hadn't she? He grabbed the helmet from her hand and looked closer. It was split in the back. Could angels forget who they were?

"No wonder you was knocked out."

It got quiet again. "Let's see what's happenin' in the world today."

She'd scooped up his paper satchel so fast he couldn't react. He looked worried as her hand jammed down into the bag. Plastic rattling sounded out he knew she'd wonder about. Her hand came out with a fat pill bottle. She read the label in a whisper, looking at him half-embarrassed and curious, shaking the near empty bottle.

Oxycontin. Her happy smile faded. "What are you doin' with these pills? Oxys?"

"Shhhh . . . give those over!" he hissed back in a panic, grabbing the bottle, glancing over his shoulder into the house. "Them's Aunt Lee's!"

"What are you doing with them then?"

He hesitated. She could tell Benny was torn about something.

"Aunt Lee has me deliver a few of them to her friends sometimes. She calls them her headache tablets."

"Benny, you shouldn't be doing this."

He liked how she said his name. She wasn't sure he was taking her seriously.

"Pills can hurt people. Especially these pills. People go to jail over this, don't you know that?"

She shoved them back down into the bag.

Benny's mouth twisted as he thought it through. This was the test, wasn't it? God's test. He'd sent her to straighten him out.

As chance would have it, the storm clouds moving in parted just enough to beam down an impressive column of sunlight, brightening the yard and Angel's pretty scratched face. She was glowing and Benny was in love and on the right side of the Lord and sorry for all the pills he'd delivered for Aunt Lee, and calling Rennie Morgan a heathen last year, and accidently looking too long at Angel's legs when he found her in the ditch, and especially sorry for all the times he'd told his Aunt how hard it was living in a "whorder" house even though she'd been good to him after his momma moved away all those years ago after the bank incident.

The lightness of her green eyes had him hypnotized.

"Maybe you're right," he stammered, feeling extra guilty. Had he failed the test and disappointed her? A familiar dread set in, the same as when he'd walked home with a sorry report card crammed down into his book bag, hoping it would somehow magically disappear.

Angel saw Benny's confusion. He looked hurt. Wasn't it strange to see someone as big and easily intimidating as him look so weak and worried? He was different for sure. Like her. Odd and probably not much bothered with to understand by people. Like her. Maybe her big plans weren't over and done after all.

"Hey, I've got a crazy idea there, Benny," she started, trying to change the subject. "How would you like to be our team manager?"

Benny blinked. She might as well have asked him if he wanted to win the Chocolate Milk for Life Sweepstakes.

"A manager? Of a roller-derby team? Me?"

She nodded with a smile, the idea growing on her. She lowered her voice. "It's a lot better than selling pills, ain't it?"

"I'd just love that," Benny gushed. "I've never managed anything before." A nervous shiver shot up his back. Was this something he'd be able to do? Was it harder than his paper route? Getting people to get taxes done or getting tans? And were there more angels just like her?

"How many of y'all are they?'

"One."

"One?" Benny was really confused now.

"How can you do all that stuff with only one person?'

"No. It's just me right now. We've got some recruiting to do. And we've got to find a track. And we need uniforms. And more skates. And helmets. And advertising. And sponsors. See why we need a manager? It's like God or something sent you my way, Benny."

Benny was smiling bigger than he had in a long time.

"Why you grinning so big?"

"I was thinking the same thing, Angel."

No Dumping

Dear Shannon Dixon,

Please find the enclosed dirty-ass diaper (one of thirty-seven-and-a-half) found in an extra-large contractor's bag of miscellaneous household trash pulled from the illegal roadside dump along the north bank of the Powelton River near Church Hill Road. The refuse of said bag also contained mail which provided your name and address. While it appears more than one bag of trash from your residence was disposed of at this illegal dump, the single bag containing the baby poop diapers was plenty enough to deal with on our end.

Interesting Fact: Did you know it takes five hundred years for a diaper to decompose? Given the general date of the mail we found, the thirty-seven diapers (and a half) had been baking in the sun and rot for two months. We hope you appreciate the endeavor our staff undertook in accomplishing this communication.

Please cease this illegal activity. You should know we are installing cameras at the site in efforts of further preventing illegal dumping at this location.

Have a safe and clean day,
Guardians of the Powelton River

Dear Dale Andrews,

Please find enclosed the approximate twenty pounds of aluminum beer and pop cans (now crushed) found in a trash bag at the illegal Powelton River dump near the intersection of River Road and Field's Lane. While we discourage illegal dumping along our waterways, we wouldn't want anyone cheated out of some good recyclable cans. There's probably a good nine dollars here, so have at it.

Interesting Fact: Did you know it can take up to four hundred years for a pop can to break down?

Please cease and desist this illegal activity. You should know we are installing cameras at the site in efforts of further preventing illegal dumping at this location.

Most Sincerely,
Guardians of the Powelton River

Dear Samuel Coleman,

Please find enclosed all of this past February, March, and April's various credit-card applications (unopened, unless already opened when thrown away by you). Needless to say, your address was found multiple times within a number of trash bags at the illegal roadside dump along the Powelton River near Church Hill Road.

Interesting Fact: Did you know that even your pet's identity can be stolen and assigned a credit card?

Please cease this illegal activity. You should know we are installing cameras at the site in efforts of further preventing illegal dumping at this location.

Here's to a safe and clean day!
Guardians of the Powelton River

Dear Albert French,

You'll find enclosed a number of empty Zig Zag candy-bar wrappers, evidence of your having dumped what must have been a surplus of outdated candy at the Powelton River illegal dump location near River Road and Cow Bend. While most of them were outdated by at least two months when we found them, they tasted just fine (though a bit mushy if a bar had been in the sun too much). Thank goodness most of the boxes you tossed over the bank were in the shade and it was early spring.

We've been eating on them for half a year now, but have plenty left from the thirteen, twenty-four count boxes. Thank you. Seriously, thank you. We found a few invoices on the packaging if you're wondering how we knew to send this correspondence to French's Tackle & Grill (love your slaw dogs, by the way).

Interesting Fact: Did you know Zig Zag candy bars have been around since 1934?

Please cease this illegal activity. You should know we are installing cameras at the site in efforts of further preventing illegal dumping at this location.

Here's to a happy Earth!
Guardians of the Powelton River

Dear Susan Anders,

Please find the enclosed box of Dollywood memorabilia. We found your contact information in a bag of trash in the illegal Powelton River dump near the intersection of River Road and Field's Lane. This much discarded memorabilia from Dollywood had to have been a mistake, so here you go. Interesting Fact: I looked up one of your more vintage souvenirs and the piece is worth about thirty dollars on eBay, so you should look into that.

Please cease this illegal activity. You should know we are installing cameras at the site in efforts of further preventing illegal dumping at this location.

To safe drinking water for all!
Guardians of the Powelton River

Dear Dale,

Please find enclosed the last three letters sent to my address by the "Guardians of the Powelton River." My ex-husband, Richard, once used that awful dump near Church Hill Road. I don't know what he uses now since I kicked his sorry ass out last month (finally!). He was a slob and a cheater and a liar. Your letters used to make him so mad he couldn't see straight (I always looked forward to them). Anyway, I just wanted to let you know that it was him and not me and it's not necessary to send any of these kinds of letters my way anymore, okay? You're probably wondering how I figured out it was you sending them, but I figure if I'm going to be member number two of the "Guardians" I need a few tricks of my own, right? Interesting Factoid: (I like to call them factoids, if you don't mind): Did you know that a third of Americans have never met their neighbors? We probably need to meet and talk out tactics and strategy. Come by some time for a cup of coffee. You know where I live. Bring one of them Zig Zags, if you got any left.

A great admirer of your work,
Rookie Guardian of the Powelton River
Annie Singleton

Hollow of the Dolls

Little Cindy imagined her momma's yells from all the way down the coal road, like they were chasing her blindly in the dark, slick through the night trees, even from this far away, determined to run her down and find her. She remembered her daddy talking about how sounds travel farther at night. But what about memories? How far do you walk to get away from remembering such awful sounds?

Her momma might have hushed on her now, but what she'd screamed at Cindy earlier that day still swirled in her confused mind, the barked insults and threats raking across the house and blasting down into Cindy's ears as hard as any whooping with a belt ever did. Some things, some voices, some awful words, never go away. Even a twelve-year-old understands that.

The way her momma made her feel when she lashed out made perfect sense in her head. But she had terrible trouble putting the right words together when she got so sad and angry, but she knew good and well what she was feeling inside. When she just couldn't say things right she'd just not talk at all. Go quiet. Sometimes for a long while.

That's probably what upset her momma most—Cindy's refusal to talk. Linda Lee was a big talker after all. Why couldn't her daughter be as well? And a yeller. And a mean old damn gossip. And an "out-and-out drunk" she'd heard her daddy scream out more than once. All those terrible things, and worse, but she was still her momma's Cindy, so she hung on best she could.

But now Little Cindy was alone out on the main road, again, damming back the tears, angry, embarrassed to cry even if no one could see them in her eyes and on her cheeks so deep in the middle of a night not even the dogs cared to stir and bark at a noise.

Things had gotten worse than usual. She'd come home from school one day not long ago, in such a good mood, only to find her momma, near falling down, "cleaning out" her room. She could hear the yells all the way to the street when she stepped off the bus, a muffled pitch of a shriek, stuff thumping around inside the house, and something about a "pig sty" and not knowing how "anyone could live like this." Her friends, Misty and Renn, walked away, embarrassed for their friend, not knowing what to say, expecting another version of the same thing tomorrow or next week. They were used to it by now.

Cindy's bedroom things covered the living room in scattered piles. Clothes, notebooks of drawings, a Mason jar of marbles busted open and rolling in every direction, a broken bag of seashells and scattered sand from their trip to the beach last year.

But what hurt her feelings and scared her most were her poor stuffed animals. Her "babies" as she affectionately knew them. They weren't piled up. They were tossed all over, a bear on the couch, another one behind the TV, a stuffed squirrel kicked half under the recliner, an octopus hanging from the fake-gold chandelier that always seemed too large for the room. She wouldn't miss the marbles and shells so much, even her sketches of dragons and elves and dinosaurs, but the stuffed animals couldn't go!

Cindy pled between sobs.

"No, momma! Where'll they go? Who'll take care of them?"

She'd raced around the living room, scooping up her babies and apologizing softly into their furry ears, nuzzling them with comforting hugs, Linda Lee drunkenly yanking them from her cradled grasp. Cindy had lost the argument, but finally talked her out of throwing away so many. Choosing was the worst. How do you choose between all your babies? And what kind of momma would make her choose which to keep and which to stuff in a garbage bag for the trash truck Friday morning, standing over her impatiently, arms crossed, scowling, as Cindy said her goodbyes to each one by name before lightly laying them face up in the bag: Silly Snake, Browny Bear, Monkey Monkey, Red Caterpillar, Blue Dog Ruff. It felt like a funeral, like when they'd buried their pit bull Sammy in the back yard by the pool. Momma had cried for three days over that dog.

Waiting for her parents to go to sleep that night was awful, like Christmas Eve and trying to stay awake. She was so sleepy by the time everything fell quiet in the house and it was safe to move. She snuck out of her room, by her momma passed out on the couch and mumbling, by her parents' bedroom, her daddy's snores and snuffles almost shaking the walls, out the front screen door and around the corner of the house to the big metal trash drums. Sometimes her daddy would use them for burning stuff. That scared her. She'd worried all day long.

Piled atop the week's garbage was the white trash bag, soft and bulging from its contents. In the glow of the streetlight she could see one of her bears, Shaggy, arching his face up against the stretching plastic as if he needed air, his eyes wide in surprise and confusion. Elfy, a Christmas elf she always placed under the tree each year, had her long wiry arm hugged around Shaggy's neck and shoulder under the straining plastic. It was nice to be hugged, Cindy thought. Even if you were suffocating in a trash bag waiting to be burnt alive.

Don't worry, she whispered so quietly it might have only been a thought.

I'm here now, my babies.

Careful as she could, hoping not to get the dogs started, she rolled the heavy bag off the bin and finger tore a few air holes in the top. Several weak sighs of relief rose from inside and she felt better. Blue Snail squirmed his slow way through the soft crush of bodies, peering a sleepy eye through one of the air holes and gave her a knowing wink.

She struggled her way down the rutted gravel drive, cradling the bag in her arms until she hit the main road, a veiny hive of coal trucks in the day, weird and quiet now in a way she hadn't imagined. She got so tired so fast she started dragging the overstuffed bag the best she could with her tiny frame, still unsure where she was bound, but determined to help her pretty babies escape the trash-truck crusher in the morning. The truck frightened her as she was waking up on Friday mornings. The robotic *whirrrrrs* and *clank-bangs* sounded like some angry cartoon war machine was just on the other side of her bedroom wall trying to claw through.

Once they knew it was her, the babies talked softly in the bag, something about making room and getting someone's elbow out of their neck and how happy they were to hear her voice again and how they'd missed her and knew they were finally safe and felt so sorry for her when her momma screamed and threatened all of them.

"It's okay," she whispered between heavy breaths, "you're all safe now."

"We know," they whispered back in happier little muffled voices. "We know, Momma."

The next morning Cindy woke to screams from outside the house along with the trash truck's groaning scariness. She jumped out of bed and spied a look out the window, seeing her momma hovering over the trash bin that was obviously empty of the bag of dolls.

"Cindy! Get your little ass out here right now! Wha'd you do with that bag of trash?"

Cindy didn't want to say too much. "What bag, Momma?" she hollered back.

"You know exactly what I'm talkin' bout, girl! Get out here!"

It wasn't an outright lie. Since she'd gotten rid of the bag before wrapping her dolls up and burying them in a shallow hole off the side of the road, technically she couldn't account for the trash bag anymore, could she? But Linda Lee fussed all morning long. Cindy missed school, stubborn in her refusal, as best as a child could, to rat out where her babies had gone. Losing the battle, her momma had marched into her room in a fit of adult helplessness and gathered up nearly all the rest of Cindy's dolls. By end of the morning, only a few were spared the greasy smolder of the trash barrel, a little Domo doll, perched lonely on Cindy's broken TV and a few others of her absolute favorites. By then, Cindy was too angry to cry.

Cindy was even quieter than usual after that, sulled up, talking just enough to get by. What pissed Linda Lee off most was catching Cindy alone in her room, the door shut up tight, her talking away in there, like how she wished her daughter would talk to her. Cindy would be in there chattering away with what remained of those damned stuffed animals. The few that her husband Bill had finally forbidden her from tossing in the fire bin that morning. He was so controlling, thinking he knew better how to raise her own child. Cindy was not even his. Hell, he couldn't even have kids. Sometimes, when she snuck up and pressed her ear flat against the locked door, she would hear Cindy's muffled voice changing back and forth, where it sounded like a real conversation with lots of people. It spooked her. She figured it was the alcohol playing tricks on her again. That happened.

It wasn't just the alcohol, though, was it? Something had turned in little Cindy, right after that last awful fight, perhaps as she was forced to choose that last round of babies for the burn bin, to watch them waste away in flames and float into the trees. It was a shift of the mind requiring words the girl would not learn for years, a twist of thoughts in abstract and confusion accepted by her young mind as natural but foreign to the tongue.

And after a while, though it made her feel awful when she noticed, she became angrier and angrier at her babies, just like how her momma was always angry with her. She loved them, yes, oh how she loved them one and all. How couldn't she? But hadn't they caused her all this terrible pain and that made her so angry she could spit rocks? She'd heard her daddy say that once. Wasn't her momma angry at her because of them? Wasn't that how people kept angry at everyone all the time, because of someone else? This was how the world worked Cindy was learning.

"A twelve-year-old's got to act her age," she'd hiss at a mirror, grimacing her face and wagging a critical finger, parroting her momma's evening time slur just low enough for no one but Domo to hear. Domo would grin his pointed tooth smile at such good impressions of the mean woman. Cindy would pace the room, circling in a silent rant, arms moving in mimicked anger, mouthing words, stumbling, throwing things. "You need to act your age . . . get rid of all these useless toys . . . you're just taking up too much space . . ."

Then it was back to the mirror, staring herself down, catching a strange familiar flash in her own eyes.

You need to grow up, Cindy.

But that seriousness would eventually break. She would sob as quietly as possible in her confusion. How could they? How could her babies—the ones she'd loved so much for so long—bring so much pain on her head from her momma? Narrowing a stare at Domo, he'd nod encouragement from whatever shelf he happened to have climbed up to that day. Cindy was forgetting where she put him. It seemed she was forgetting a lot of things these days, was surprised to find Domo in such odd places, way up under the bed, on a top shelf she couldn't quite reach, on the window sill staring out at the night. She'd bend down and look over his squared tiny shoulders, sure she could see with him, through the black-beaded shine of his plastic eyes, down the drive toward the coal road.

More and more she snuck out after midnight and tip-toed her way down that road, careful not to set off the dogs, her slight and quiet features dodging lamplight, trying to be lost in the roadside shadow. After all these weeks she had the nighttime walk down to less than ten minutes. She could almost do it with her eyes closed, with Domo, twine-strapped over her neck and shoulder like a purse, always helping her walk, watching for potholes and copperheads on the night road. Domo was always more than happy to go. He was, after all, her last and only friend.

Once to her destination, it was off the gravel and across the muddy ditch line and a few feet up the lightless hillside, blindly digging out the soggy and blackening quilt holding her cache of animals and the stolen bag of supplies, a hammer and a heavy paper bag of long, rusting carpentry nails.

As she readied for the quick night's work, spreading the heavy mud away with her hands, that scary feeling would overtake her, like someone was watching her from behind, studying on her movements and judging. Then she'd stand in the dark, claw-headed hammer swinging loosely at the end of her arm, the other hand fingering the sharp fang of a two-inch nail. She'd pace, talk with her hands, whisper just loud enough for the animals to hear, a strange familiar feeling gurgling up, throwing in a slur and a stagger, Domo crawling up and grinning over her hunched shoulder, encouraging, directing into her ear, into her thoughts, her sight.

"Which one's it gonna be tonight?" Cindy would demand in a vacant voice.

"They won't answer, I bet," Domo would challenge, glaring down on the pile of molding, soggy dolls.

The nights of unburying her babies carefully from their sleep, reassuring them, hugging their soft damp necks were over.

"You all choose," she'd hiss, her body arched over the stuffed animals like a starved buzzard over carrion. This was her constant hiss now, laying the remaining babies out in a row on the fresh ground, forcing them to choose amongst themselves.

No one said a word. None made a move. Not a flinch. By now they knew better.

But a few eyes locked on Elmer, one of Cindy's stuffed bears, all pink and blue eyes with a red ribbon around his neck, now impaled through the shoulder with a long nail to the nearest roadside telephone pole, his long fur cornering off and down like ice cycles of matting with each new rain. Below him was the limp brown body of Moosey, mildewing, his antlers soaked heavy and wilted, one eye popped off, a nail squared through his chest. To Moosey's left was the blue unicorn, Tinker, her single similarly wilting horn mirrored with a nail spiked through the forehead, hoofed legs sprawled and stiff in surprise. Others hung quietly with them, given up and offering no protest.

The dolls on the ground stole glances up at their friends' silhouettes, then snuck a glance to Cindy as she worked. It was so confusing now, living in the ground. Waiting. And while that person looked like Cindy's form, mostly all they could make out was someone else's scary mumbling voice connected to the fumbling in the dark, the sudden clumsy pounding of nails, a curse in the night. Then another friend spiked and hanging.

Where had their Cindy gone?

But down deep they knew they'd never see her again and they wondered why someone resembling Cindy's momma, the one they'd all escaped from, was now coming at nights and hurting them.

Uncle Archie Goes
One for Three

Uncle Archie constantly went on about how the shop lacked
certain *must haves*.

"I've been around the world enough to know what an odd shop
needs, boy," he preached at me, "and we're mightily lacking in some
respects."

All I could do was nod and agree when he got like this. How
could I help much given the limited access to the outside world I
had as a young teenager with no license and bald tires on my bike.
Nevertheless he'd remind me how a "world of adventure" was right
off the steps of the front porch. He'd reinforce this lesson by having
me regularly watch for special items to round out his collection:
a legit mummy (Egyptian or South American), a stuffed alligator
for the roof (long enough to be seen from Flat Hill Road), a lock of
hair from Princess Di, and a chupacabra (North or South American, but European if necessary).

I tried, but I never happened across any of those treasures on my
weekend yard-sale rounds or when digging in random household
discards on the road, though I did have him going once when I
pulled a wad of hair from the sink drain and placed it in a sandwich

bag. The gag was up though when he noticed how many different colors of hair was in the sample.

After all the world traveling Uncle Archie did I figured he would have acquired at least one of these "unicorn finds," as he knew them, by this time in his collecting. "It's a matter of cost, boy, not just geographic luck and fateful timing. Not only are these items near impossible to find, they ain't cheap to come by."

Uncle Archie eventually checked off one of those illusive items. As luck would have it, we got a break on the chupacabra front the summer I turned fourteen. It wasn't all good luck, though. *Chupacabras* are mysterious crypto-zoological creatures known to harbor ill fortune, and not just for delicious goats since their name means "goat-sucker."

Dad and I knew something was up when we opened the shop as usual one Saturday morning and got smacked in the nose with the foul and partly familiar odor of Uncle Archie at work. The store smelled of rubbing alcohol, beer, wet dog, and human sweat, but not in that order. We heard him in the back room struggling with something.

"It smells like a wet dog slept in the store all night and didn't get let out in time for its business," Dad yelled to the back.

"I've been in here all night working!" Uncle Archie yelled back. "And don't get personal, little brother!" he joked.

As we entered the back workroom where "all the magic happens," as Uncle Archie often bragged, it was immediately apparent where the ripeness originated. As a mostly self-taught taxidermist, my uncle hadn't learned all the discipline he might have in a classroom setting. A more focused professional would have neatly disposed of the guts of the creature he now had hanging half in and half out of the giant specimen jar in the middle of the room. The animal was more or less bent in the middle, folded over the rim of the glass since it had no innards. It looked like a deflated furry balloon. Its head and torso and front legs were submerged in the usual clear watery liquid, its ass-end facing my uncle who was struggling a might bit to hoist the body's remainders. At a glance it looked like he was trying to drown a starved and rabid mangy dog.

Several empty gallon jugs labeled isopropyl alcohol were scattered in the floor. My eyes burnt from the raw alcohol scent and the tangled guts already rotting on the stainless-steel worktable. That mixed with Uncle Archie's ripeness after a night of work was taking my breath. Dad was struggling, too.

"What the hell is that thing?" Dad asked, wiping a tear from his eye. "Is it rotten?"

"No, it's actually pretty darn fresh. I think the stench is from what it eats. I'm gonna have to burn these clothes, I betcha. It was pretty bad opening the thing up to gut it. That's plain to see, huh?"

"What . . . is . . . it?"

I closed in on the glass for a better look, the thing's face floating mere inches from mine.

The clear solution and glass were probably altering the appearance of the creature, but I could tell it was crazy looking enough not to need much help. Its eyes were wide-open and staring. Its mouth snarled wide-open like it was howling at the moon in its last wild moments, exposing more teeth than I've ever seen in dog's mouth—if it was a dog—its canines stretched long and sharp and slanted and deformed. Its elongated tongue lolled out from the corner of its mouth. Its body looked almost hairless, like it was set with the bad mange, but without all the sores, and what hair it had was black and wiry at its joints and it had a strip of long spiky mane down its stretched neck and knobby back. Its ribs showed like it was winter starved. It had paws tipped with broken claws. Its tail was long, hairless, and pointed.

I knew what it was.

"Uncle Archie!" I gasped. "Where in the world did you find a chupacabra?"

Literally. Where in the world, I wondered.

I was so excited.

He whispered as though there might be shoppers already in the story who'd overhear. "Best you all not know such things. The dark crypto-zoology trade is a mysterious underworld of back-stabbing bastards and villains. I don't want y'all involved."

Whenever he switched over into his spy-vs-spy mode of topic avoidance I could tell there was something fishy afoot. He gave me a wink and changed the subject. I was disappointed. I never knew what to believe in this family.

"Boy, why don't you grab a construction bag and get these remainders slopped up and stored in the Deepfreeze and then spray some air freshener in the store before someone walks in and loses their breakfast."

He was bad for never throwing anything away.

"Good idea. I'd end up cleaning it up," I mumbled.

"Help me push the rest of this body over the rim, brother," he implored of Dad. "Must weigh over a hundred pounds even dressed out." The whole body plopped down fully submerged and cradled around the smoothness of the glass like a bulky serpent and kept coasting forward for a few seconds like it knew what it was doing before coming to a stop like a sleeping fish. It was staring at me again, still unblinking. A series of noxious bubbles escaped the corner of its dead grin and popped at the surface of the liquid.

"Hope it keeps its eyes open like that. People need to get their money's worth."

"We're keeping all this?" I asked with a grimace, sloshing a gloved handful into a bag hoping the bottom wouldn't drop out.

"Heck. You know what ten feet of Chupacabra intestines goes for on the trade market?" he asked, as if I should know better than to question the obvious.

I didn't know.

"Me either. If you figure it out, let me know. See if it's on the Google somewhere."

A lot of times I'd just make something up to make him feel better. A hundred and fifty Euros a pound sounded good to me. He'd probably never bother looking it up himself.

The family woke up even earlier than usual on Monday morning to the racket of Uncle Archie's table saw and hammering. He'd managed to quietly dig the twelve-by-twelve-footer in twilight, but couldn't hold off on the noisier aspects of construction any longer. He was good with a pick and shovel. He had, after all, tunneled the fallout shelter now used as the Underground Reunion. A little footer was nothing, even if the sun wasn't all the way up.

"It's a new room to house that vampire-dog," he told us.

"El Chupacabra," I said.

"Goat-sucker. Mangy vamp dog. Bipedal livestock folk serial murderer. Don't matter the name right now. Besides, we're gonna have a contest to give it a name other than its mythological moniker."

"Like Bill?"

"I hope it's better than that, boy."

"We charging to see it since it'll have its own room?"

"Yep. You got the right idea. It better bring good money, too," he grumbled. "This here thirty-gallon show jar alone cost us 150 dollars."

Funny how when it came to money everything had to do with "us."

We celebrated the "Deadly Den of the Mountain Chupacabra" with a soft opening a month later on a Saturday morning to a great turn out. Fifty dollars went a long way toward getting us a good quarter-page ad in the *Labor County Weekly Trader*. After some haggling with the paper's layout advisor, we'd settled on a picture of the big glass jar with the contents pixelated out and Uncle Archie, of course, standing by the jar looking concerned for his safety. There was a coupon cutout portion of the add guaranteeing fifty cents off a three-dollar admission if the bearer filled out the provided dotted line with a possible name for the new attraction.

While Deadly Den of the Mountain Chupacabra wasn't our first choice as a name for the new draw, it's what we settled on finally as a family. We tossed around variations involving Every Goat's Nightmare, Sasquatch's Bloodthirsty Canine Cousin, and The Appalachian Mange Vampire. We all had our favorites, but we settled on simplicity.

The "Den" was low lit to make up for there not being much more in the room than the creature. The specimen jar was about two-and-a-half-feet tall. Even so, it possessed a certain sinister mood. The jar stood on a square-topped stainless-steel rolling table in the center of the room. The whole scene looked very scientific, as if doctors would come in any minute and roll the monster away for new tests. A red velvet rope kept the tourists at arm's length from the glass.

Uncle Archie had rigged up a big rubber mallet on a hinge so that when a line was yanked at the checkout counter, a heavy thump rumbled through the floor of the Den. It scared the tour-goers something awful, vibrating up through their feet, making the animal shift in its distorted watery quarters like it was coming back for vengeance. It was typical Uncle Archie Hollywood genius.

Besides running tickets and jerking that mallet rope, my other job for the first month was collecting suggested names for the creature as patrons left the store. This usually meant deciphering some pretty atrocious handwriting. Most of the participants were children so this made the task that much more difficult. I'd never seen so many heart-dotted *i*'s since. Seems adults weren't too interested in the game.

Maybe they sensed it was rigged from the start. I was worried with the results at first. "Spot" had a long lead early in the month, but a few other names caught up fast and turned it into a real contest. "Killer," "Choopy," "Fanger," and "Mangy" made it a strong top five list by midmonth. Unfortunately for creativity's sake, Uncle Archie had been calling the animal "Ed" since he'd brought him in and no one was changing his mind.

We tried to express just how unfrightening "Ed the Chupacabra" would be.

"Fine," he relented. "Eduardo it is."

"Eduardo" successfully doubled our business at the Odditorium & Gifts for a few months that summer, which pleased Archie since that more than paid for the room addition expenses. He'd tell me, "You gotta spend it to make it, but don't spend too much." Everything after a few good months of summer traffic to the new attraction was sausage gravy, he bragged. A good profit, in other words.

Days were a steady stream of curiosity seekers, people from town or in the county. Some passing through from off the freeway. It could be anyone. Families on vacation. Businesspeople traveling through looking to kill some time. Busloads of grade schoolers on field trips. After a few years in the shop I'd gotten pretty good at figuring out what a person's interests might be once they spent a few minutes in the store. You can size people up pretty fast by paying attention. That's a good thing for preventing shoplifting, too.

For instance, along the end of summer this one man came in the shop and I got a vibe from him. I could tell this one wasn't real fascinated with taxidermy art, or jars of wet specimens, or taking a tour of the Underground Reunion. His eyes never stayed on one item long enough to sufficiently see what he was looking at. He was only acting like he was "kicking tires." Something was up.

I glanced at our TV monitor hooked to our security cameras. The images weren't terribly clear, but the ten-pack of shop cameras Uncle Archie bought off eBay made the place look like the lobby of Fort Knox (though he always told me there wasn't any gold there anymore). If the guy was thinking about stealing at least we'd have something.

He eventually wandered back near "Eduardo's" room. We had it curtained off now with nice thick green velvet pullback curtains. They were closed. Just as he was about to peek through, I interrupted his nosiness.

"Excuse me, sir! You'll have to purchase a ticket for that room!"

He then walked back up to the counter, deliberate-like. He had on a dark suit. White dress shirt, thin black tie. He seemed friendly.

"Hi there, young man. May I ask if Archie Parker might be here?"

I told him he was out back working.

"Can I help you?"

"Well, can I speak with him? I haven't seen him in a long time."

I figured they were friends.

I yelled to the back. "Uncle Archie! Someone for you!"

He came up grumbling from being disturbed.

"Archie Parker?" the man asked.

"Can I help you?" It didn't seem like Uncle Archie knew the guy after all.

"You *are* the owner of Eduardo back there, the quote/unquote, chupacabra, correct?"

He made air quotes in the air when he said *chupacabra*.

Uncle Archie hesitated, but slowly responded. "Yes, I am . . . how can we help you?"

"Well . . ." the man started, reaching into his coat pocket.

Uncle Archie stepped back and shoved an arm in front of me. "Whoa there, mister! There's no need for violence!" I jumped back, startled. (I guess Uncle Archie was thinking the man was pulling a gun.)

But it was an envelope, not a gun. An official-looking envelope. Sealed. With a bunch of names in a row on the letterhead. The man tossed it onto the checkout counter in front of us like it was a hot potato and he was glad to get rid of it.

"You've been served, sir," the man stated with a grin of satisfaction, very matter-of-factly.

"Say what?" Uncle Archie asked, stunned, picking up the envelope.

"You're being sued, sir. By one Thelma Chandler. Good day."

And with that the man walked out. I watched him walk through the door and off the porch and across the parking lot. He didn't leave in a car; he was on foot. I watched him walk until he disappeared around the bend of the road.

Ms. Thelma Chandler had brought her grandkids to the Odditorium about a month earlier. I dug out their entries for naming the creature. Four-year-old Sid wanted to name it "Elmo" and six-year-old Amy wanted to name it "Brownie Boy." Thelma had entered as well, but with an added statement: "Percy—The creature looks strangely like my poor lost dog, only with much less hair. I miss him so. Please name it Percy."

According to the lawsuit, Ms. Chandler was convinced that "Eduardo" was her "poor lost dog." He'd gone missing some months back and she assumed it was lost forever, but after seeing our animal she was beyond convinced that the mystery was solved. Uncle Archie had found her precious Percy. Praise the heavens and Amen. But she wasn't thrilled since the animal was now dead and swimming in alcohol behind glass. She was convinced he'd either stolen Percy from somewhere, killed Percy outright, or found the body out there in the countryside somewhere. As far as she was concerned, the carcass belonged to her for a proper dispositioning.

Uncle Archie was appalled.

"That's ridiculous! Of all the gall! She wants him back. But that's my chupacabra, fair and square! She can go out and fetch her own."

We reminded him that, though we were family and believed him, he'd never gone into much detail yet on the actual acquisition of the specimen.

"Indeed, I have not," he agreed. "To keep you all out of the complication of the dark world of crypto-zoological trading. It can be a dangerous world, case in point." He shook the lawsuit paperwork at us.

"But I will tell you a little something." He leaned in closer. "I didn't steal it from nowhere or no one. I didn't pay anything for it. And it was dead when I loaded it in the truck." Then he gave us a wink.

All those hints only made Dad all the more curious. Of course it was killing me.

"Well, you say it was dead when you loaded it in the truck. What about right before that?" Dad asked.

"Yeah," I added.

"Hmmm. Let me try to remember," he stalled. "I do remember it was dark. The middle of the night. I doubt the thing belonged to that Chandler woman since she lives out on the east side of the county and I ran into this mangy thing on the opposite side. That's a lot of territory to run and survive."

"And?" I asked.

"Well, I ran into him. Literally. I hit him with the truck."

Uncle Archie looked a little ashamed.

"You killed it?"

"Not immediately. It took a while. I tried to save him best I could. A live one's much better than a dead one, don't you think?"

We nodded. You couldn't argue with that.

"Well, I was coming around Mullins Bend when I saw the bugger in my headlights. I about pooped myself, to tell the truth. It was standing on its hind legs in the middle of the road chewing on a possum like a salted-and-buttered ear of fresh corn. I thought it was a giant raccoon at first. Those red eyes. Jeez. They hypnotized me for a second. I didn't hit the brakes fast enough, so before I knew it, I'd hit him. He let out the awfullest howl you've never heard."

"Then what?" I demanded.

"Well, it was sort of a blur—literally a red blur when he let go of that half-eaten possum and it splattered on my windshield—but I'm pretty sure he flipped over the car. At least that's where I found him. He didn't fly on his own accord. They're not known for wings."

"Then what?" Dad demanded.

"Well, I checked my shorts and then I crept around looking for whatever it was. I found it. It was a big dog, kind of, good ol' 'Eduardo,' sort of hairless, ribs all showing like it was starving. Big rows of teeth snarling at me. Paws with those big claws grabbing out. Blood and slobber flying everywhere. I put a blanket over it its head and it calmed down and I tried to help it, but there wasn't anything I could do. I sure wasn't gonna give it mouth-to-mouth after it was chewing on that possum. All I knew at that point was I'd found me a chupacabra sure as the world. It died and I dragged it up into the bed of the truck and came home. Simple."

"Simple," Dad repeated.

We didn't know what more to say to any of that. What could we?

Uncle Archie went into town to talk to a lawyer friend the next day. He said he had a plan for avoiding a court battle he knew he could win, but only after months of stress and money better spent on the shop.

"Mediation, boy," he told me. "Mediation before adjudication. It's cheaper and more civil than relinquishing your fate to your peers, believe me."

Things were working out within a few days. It was a mighty tug-of-war, Uncle Archie claimed, but he figured the Odditorium was mostly the winner since the animal ended up staying with us. Ms. Chandler was given free visitation rights for her and her grandchildren and other close kin, and as hard as it was to swallow, Uncle Archie agreed to change the creature's name from "Eduardo" to "Percy." Her only other deal breaker required we unseal the creature from its jar so "Percy" could forever wear one of his old blinged-out leather collars, a black one with fake diamonds spelling out his name in pretty cursive.

"It doesn't matter if it's really her old dog or not, boy. What matters is there's still a chupacabra in a big jar back there in that room of ours," Uncle Archie confided to me.

Thelma picked Uncle Archie up for their first date the next Friday evening. Apparently mediation is sometimes the route to go.

The Clown Brothers Eller

It never fails. Every time I take my nephews off my sister's hands for a bit and go for a drive they beg me to go out the winding roads on Jamison Mountain and, of course, that means eventually rumbling over the Eller Bridge. I think they really just want to go over that bridge. It's the spot for a big "haint" story, and that's whether it's coming Halloween or not.

That's all I'll hear about once they get in the car. "We *are going the Eller Bridge way*, right Uncle Roger?" "Yeah. Aren't we?"

Sure enough, I'll take them. Heck, I like going as much as they do.

So there we'll be in the middle of the day, pulled over on this big concrete state bridge, not a thing around looking spooky at all, me telling this wild story for the thousandth time to these wide-eyed kids like they've never heard it in their lives. They just giggle their asses off and go on like the sun's down, it's a full moon, and they've spotted that giant plastic clown head bobbing down the rapids of the creek under this haunted bridge. They're a good audience, I tell ya. No wonder we've never made it all the way to Jamison Mountain.

Now the wacked-out ice cream van at the center of this tale carried all manner of cold sugary treats like any ice cream truck would and should, but this one was run by a couple of aspiring brother entrepreneurs. They were the Eller twins, Ron and Jake Eller.

They ran their route out along the beltline side of Labortown up to the rusted-out sawmill by that no name creek snaking into the west side of town and then ran zigzag along the avenues wherever the sweet fates and a few waving sweaty summer dollars would lure them. The Eller brothers weren't discriminating against anyone's money. They'd go anywhere to make a dime, you can't take that from them.

Twins they were, indeed, but some hard-living years had run havoc all over both Ron and Jake and pretty much turned them into different-looking people, though they could still pass for brothers, or at least close cousins. But up-close it was always obvious enough.

Ronnie, as everyone called him that knew him pretty good, was missing most of his left ear and a few lower teeth. Somewhat oppositely, Jake was missing some uppers along with most of his right eyebrow which was mostly scar tissue. Both injuries were inflicted upon each other during a teenage fight they both regretted, but talked up as war wounds in a sense, usually ignoring in the dramatic telling that they'd done it to each other. They mostly told people it all happened during a fight and left it at that. This story of injuries might have sounded quite gratuitous unless you knew them, and then you'd have wondered how they hadn't managed more damage on each other and them only twelve at the time. One might also have wondered how the two of them, with the way they ran their mouths, hadn't accumulated more obvious injuries the number of times they'd been in and out of county lockup.

But as they got older they got along swimmingly, swearing they'd

never taste the flesh of a brother in murderous anger again, especially since they were fancying up and becoming professional clown
ice cream experts. And they weren't just sticking a toe in and testing
the waters, as some claimed they were doing, like it was some side
hobby, like they'd go running back off to the mines if the economy
ever got back on its feet. No, this was their dream.

Selling ice cream dressed as seasonal clowns.

It was a weird-ass gig they were running for sure and it creeped
out a lot of people, but the kids would walk barefoot over smashed
torch-heated glass for a melting Frosty Choco Cone that was giving
up the ghost on a summer day, so they always had some business
somewhere. "Best not get between a husky little kid and his fifty-
cent Vanilla Moose Cone," Ronnie would warn. "That's straight up
money to be made right there. Add a clown to the mix and we'll
retire in a few years."

Ronnie, a died in the wool Nascar and *Fast and Infamous* film
fan, insisted on being behind the wheel, of course. Jake, who hadn't
had a license in years, took up the responsibility of stiff-arming
treats out of the sliding Plexiglas window to the screaming kids and
few reluctant adults who seemed to feel it was necessary to chaper-
one their kids when the Ellers rolled around.

Jake was hard of hearing, even though Ronnie was the one short
a full ear, and yelled over the muffler-less generator hanging crooked
off the back of their vehicle. It was a mostly yellow ex–U-Haul van
with the old labeling working through the spray-paint job they'd
rendered on it. That generator stunk of oil and diesel fumes and
though missing most of its muffler after the first time they got rear-
ended, even that noise had to compete with the piped-out midi-file
music mostly playing Christmas tunes all year. It had an odd rate
of speed like a dying battery, but more like the depressed heart of a
doomed endeavor. "Silent Night" was a favorite. Spooky, but familiar. But "I Want a Hippopotamus for Christmas" really sounded

like a clown tune, slower than usual, as if sung by a confused drunken man. Boy did it bring the kids out.

To up their odds at success, they'd taken a loan for three hundred big ones from their Uncle Leaman to get this dream going. They'd splurged on a few items. It was early March in their first year of business, and Ronnie, the self-realized brains of the operation, decided some diversification was in order and that Easter was an ideal time to rollout "Operation: Clown Theme Months." Jake wasn't happy with that name, but Ronnie, who was thirteen seconds older, outvoted him with enthusiasm.

Their first purchase with that fat roll of investment cash was a couple of full-bodied Easter-bunny costumes they found at the Jenkin's Flea Market over the Tennessee line in Able County. In fact, they didn't just find these hardly used jewels, they got super lucky and found a few sets of outfits for October as well. Pumpkin-headed scarecrows and devils along with some elf outfits for the Christmas season.

Yes, they were planning for operations well up into winter. They'd stacked a set of snow tires and chains in the back if needed. People still ate ice cream come cold weather, didn't they? If they ate ice cream in the warm comfort of their kitchen, it wasn't that far to the curb. They just had to figure on how to convince people to come out of their houses in the cold and walk to the roadside. Besides, it would be a waste of all that good Christmas music using it only for the Christmas parade, wouldn't it?

All of this only set them back sixty bucks, so they felt like pretty successful investors right off the bat. They figured a trip to Corville for the other months and they'd have the costume basics in order. Add their special touch of clown features to every outfit and the Eller Brothers would be in business.

As for their immediate challenge of the Easter ice cream season, you could visit a depressed looking giant bunny at the mall any time. Sit in its lap and tell it what you wanted from the little baby Jesus come Easter morning, but add some clown makeup to those long droopy ears, a little frowny mouth, and some neon whiskers. Maybe some oversized buckteeth. Tape a few pastel-colored eggs on the van side. Play the old silent game. Kids and parents alike, and even people who hated ice cream would come out to see what the hell was happening down on the corner where the crowd was gathering up. The creep factor was a natural element Ronnie and Jake brought these harmless, revered holidays.

It wasn't easy at first. If no one came running from the music and them sitting in place for five minutes, Ronnie would have Jake hop out and do a jumpy little jig around the van to get some attention. That would usually bring people out. It was solid entertainment. The floppy bunny feet were something else, but the red clown nose on the rabbit face set off the whole outfit.

They'd found their niche, though they argued on the pronunciation of the word *niche*. Ronnie insisted on pronouncing the *e*.

Every month was a challenge. On Valentine's Day, let's say, they'd wield tiny bows and arrows, draw little red broken hearts on their cheeks, wear bald caps along with their flaccid wings. Ronnie had wired up a crane system for Jake to hang from off the back of the truck to look like a flying angel between stops, but he'd gone unconscious within a few blocks from the fumes and Jake had called that experiment quits.

Their list of holiday themes could stretch over every month if they played it right: Earth Day, Memorial Day, D-Day, Fourth of July, 9/11. Harvest time they would wear the generic autumn-time pumpkin-headed scarecrows on account of their mother Linda Gene's love of fall. Thanksgiving: the old pilgrim and Indian routine. For Halloween, their favorite time, it would be matching devil goblin clown outfits for now. They promised to trade off who was who every year. Christmas: demented elves.

They knew they'd hit something big when *The Labor County Times*, the local weekly paper, inquired for an interview. Free advertising sounded great. The paper's only journalist, Susan, a dogged reporter known for her investigative talent since the mass food-poisoning incident at the Lucky Freeze Drive-In in 2014, only accompanied them for half an hour, however. It seems that while riding along with the brothers a heretofore undiscovered carsickness tendency made itself known and half the ride was spent with the poor girl's head sticking out of the serving window trailing stomach acid down the already fading paint job with Ronnie driving as fast as he could to get her to the local clinic before Jake's weak and sympathetic gag reflex followed suit and he'd end up cleaning up for both of them all evening and ruining his only Easter Bunny outfit and here it was not even Good Friday yet. Her article was pretty generic since she was too green to pay much attention to the stops they made and her head was swimming too much to take many notes. Nevertheless a few kids mentioned seeing them in the paper, so it was worth it. One kid even pointed out where the stomach acid had eaten a splattered streak of paint down to the naked metal.

Easter went off without much of a hitch. The very end of April was spent in celebration of Earth Day, so Earth Week it was. Jake's face was dark green except for the big white clown circles around his eyes and mouth and an extra-large foam nose he'd spray painted light green, and the penciled in eyebrow which was embarrassingly necessary.

He'd ventured down to the Hobby Shed and gotten a bunch of fake vine and wrapped his torso in it so he looked sort of like what he found on the internet called a "Green Man," only his was a clown version in overalls along with his normal pink afro wig. It was such a complicated outfit he often just slept in it and would redo his makeup as needed (which was about every third day).

Ronnie went with some lighter colors. A light green face with dark circles around his eyes and mouth and a dark nose. A kind of carbon copy opposite of his brother. His vines made him look like he was grown into the makings of the van cab, like a puppet controlled by wild Kudzu or poison vine or something. The kids loved it. The more the word got around the more they hauled ass out of their homes with mommy and daddy's loose change for Choco Cones and Icey-Pops just to see what this month's Eller weirdness might be. The kids would just barely grab their ice creams from Jake and let out a yell and go running like he was a zoo animal or something. Of course, the brothers loved it as much as the kids. Earth week went so well they turned May into Earth month whether or not it was an official holiday.

But there was a cloud of anxiety hanging over the Ellers during all this initial success. Uncle Leaman fancied himself a bit of a mountain mafia type. You see, he wanted double his loan back by the end of the calendar year.

The boys were doing pretty good, but they resented the hell out of Uncle Leaman being a jerk like that and they could be procrastinators. Leaman knew this. He decided that as the end of the year was coming on and it was hitting the end of September and since their "9/11 Memorial Ice Cream Month" was going pretty well, that a little incentivizing was in order for the boys.

Carp Dandridge was not only a food inspector for the county, he was a sheriff's constable to boot. Leaman had managed to keep Carp, who was a distant cousin in the family, off the Eller's backs while he had money involved. He knew there wasn't an inch of that van that could pass an inspection of any sort, let alone one for cleanliness when it came to food and beverages.

But the closer the time came for six hundred dollars to show up in Leaman's hand, the more he was tempted to remind Carp of old Ronnie and Jake's little dream.

"Why don't you go pay the boys a little visit and see if they'd prefer a food inspection any time soon. Tell 'em Uncle Leaman said, hey."

"Sure will. I was cravin' some nice cold ice cream anyways," Carp answered with no little hint of menace in his voice.

Ronnie's first reaction was to abandon the long line of kiddies Jake was attending to and stomp the shit out of the gas when he saw the squad car pull up so close behind the van. That Deputy Carp was out of the car so fast, eye-balling the back of the truck and scribbling in his notebook, it made him double nervous. Jake hadn't seen the trouble yet being occupied with the kids. He always was the clueless one. Carp was always the do-gooder in high school. At least up to tenth grade. That was the last the twins had seen of school.

Ronnie watched Carp's head cock crooked like the generator and give a satisfied grin. Then more scribbling. What had he seen? He tapped on the van with his pen, like he was inspecting the paint job. Another note. Kicked the half-bald tire. Note. He even leaned closer to the side of the van and gave a sniff. Note.

But then it happened. Through all the chocolate and vanilla and strawberry Icey-Pops and diesel and gas and oil fumes and body odor and rust and anything else floating around in the day's summer heat, that constable nose picked up something in the dead windless air that made Carp stop and give another long inquisitive sniff.

Ronnie saw him do it. Close his eyes and inhale. Then sniff again. Then an eyebrow arched like he suddenly knew something. Ronnie's foot almost went to the floor. He wanted to be down the street faster than Carp could take the next two steps to his driver's side window, but the van wasn't even running.

"Howdy, Ronnie!"

Too late.

"Well, hey there, Officer Dandridge!"

"That is you in there, ain't it? Behind all that patriotic clown get up?"

"It's me," Ronnie laughed, behind red, white, and blue stripes up and down his face with a flag stuck behind his one good ear like a pen, and a long white tangled Uncle Sam goatee he'd grown out for the month's occasion.

"Now, Ronnie, you know you can call me Carp. We're family."

"Well, alright. If you say so . . . Officer Carp. Been a while, huh?"

"Yep."

He looked around inside, past Ronnie, nosey like.

The kids gave out a big squeal and Jake wasn't doing anything to settle them down. He was honking his hand horn after each sale, yelling out, "Who's next?" *Honka! Honka!*

"Can we help you with some ice cream today? We'll let you skip line," he sort of whispered. "We know you've got lots of places to get to."

The insider's smile Ronnie offered didn't feel convincing.

Carp glanced up at the two-foot-tall clown head the boys had bought off the Jimmy Burger when it went out of business. He huffed a half laugh remembering all the dates he'd taken there when he was younger and how there was probably burger specks still in its crevices where him and the boys would chuck their leftovers at it on top of the building when no one was watching. The girls loved that stunt.

"Well, lookey there. That's the clown head from the Jimmy Burger drive-in, ain't it?"

"Yep, sure is."

"Hope it's attached good," Carp sniped, making another long note. "Oh, by the way, Leaman sends his regards, Ronnie."

That's all Ronnie had to hear. He swallowed hard, noticing Bertrand's eyes scanning an upside down flopped ice cream on the floorboard melting.

"You're not playing constable right now are ya, Carp? You're here as the food inspector, aren't you?"

"Yep. Reckon I am. If I have to be. And I'm *always* the constable, Ronnie."

"I reckon he wants something, huh?"

"Who? Leaman? Yep."

"We ain't got it. Much at least."

"Would you rather me be tearing this here van apart with a magnifying glass?"

"No."

Bertrand sniffed again, curious like, this time working his nose with an offended twist.

"Jake? How's them kids doing back there, buddy?" Jake didn't answer. He was laughing away with the kids and parents.

"Ronnie, what's that odor I'm smelling? I catch a whiff of it every now and again."

"What? Hmmm. Oh, it's probably that generator back there's all," Ronnie laughed, inching for the ignition.

"No. It smells like, um, what is it? Um . . . cat piss, Ronnie. Ya know? That sort of smell. But more toxic smelling. It's real strong . . . coming from your window right here."

"Jake! We've got to go!"

Carp was taking a step back now, in a defensive stance, no longer the food inspector and fully in constable mode, a shaky hand hovering on his Taser sidearm. He knew what was up.

"Now cousin, you know as well as I do you're shakin' up some

meth back in that van. Puttin' all those kids in danger. I'm surprised you ain't blowed up by now with all the fumes."

Ronnie turned the engine over with a cough and rumble and
gunned it in neutral. "Jake! Wrap it up!"

Carp aimed the Taser right between Ronnie's eyes.

"Turn that engine off and let's talk about this. Let's let a little
money owed to Leaman be the worst of it, okay?"

Jake's patriotic face popped up suddenly beside his brothers in
the cab about the time Carp pull the trigger.

"Oh, hi Bertrand! Whoa! Holy shit!"

The brothers ducked and the Taser anchor lodged into the dash-
board leather with a spark. Ronnie hit the gas blindly, Jake hollered
as he lost balance and flipped back into the van with a thud and
crash, and all Carp could do was kick streaks down the van with a
pointy boot toe as it swerved off. No kids were injured in the ensu-
ing mayhem. The Taser gun dragged and bounced back and forth
between the side of the van and the asphalt until it wrapped around
a stop sign Ronnie ran down the street and cut loose.

A few blocks later and Labortown was in the midst of its most
exciting car chase in years.

Ronnie was surprised the old van had it in it as they tore hell
down Cumberland Street, a straight shot toward the eastern mountains where they might could ditch the van and run off. Carp, on
the other hand, would have done the same and wasn't giving up an
inch, but also didn't want to push them so much as to cause them
to wreck and explode with whatever half-assed lab they had cooked
up in back. Too many unknowns.

It must have gotten out on the scanners. By the time they were
blowing the red light at the Pic-and-Run, a crowd was gathering
up, including Susan from the newspaper, and people were waving
like the van was full of victorious football players returning from

an away game with a police escort but at fifty-seven miles an hour in a thirty-five zone. Jake thought it'd be funny to throw ice creams since he and Ronnie were headed to prison anyway, so every time they shot past a crowd he'd toss a box of product to lighten the load and wave an American flag for effect.

When one of the boxes made Carp swerve it gave him an idea so he punched his clown-gloved fist through a back window and chucked frozen boxes out like bombs. The first box of Choco Cones was just short of doing the job, rolled awkwardly, and hit the curb, but the second smacked just right, bounced, and slid up the squad car's front hood and shattered the passenger-side windshield. Jake, not one to normally use their "alternative goods," paused a moment, struck up a blunt, and took a big hit, and then, since everything in their world was disintegrating around them, got ballsy, bent down, undid the chains on the near worthless generator, and gave the back double doors a heavy boot which knocked it off its crooked shelf and into Carp's path. It missed for all the effort.

But then the first shot rang out.

"Ronnie! He's shootin' at us! Carp's shootin' at us!"

Jake stumbled up to the front, wide-eyed and worried. "With his gun!"

"He's only trying to flatten the tires, Jake!"

"I don't want to go to prison, Ronnie! Oh no! Oh no! And here in the middle of 9/11 Month!"

"Calm down, Jakey Boy! Keep throwing shit! Keep your head about ya!"

"I'll try!" Jake yelled stumbling into the back.

"And watch those cook pots!"

Another shot and a ricochet off something metal.

Jake ducked while grabbing a box of Stawberry-A-GoGo-Bars

and heaved them out the back like a block of ice. Then it was an entire box of American flags. Another gunshot shattered the van's other back window, glass flying everywhere. Jake answered by tossing out two gigantic Styrofoam pumpkin heads and a full box of multicolored oversized pull-on slippers. Jake had no idea where they'd come from.

"Guess that takes care of our plans to surprise Momma for fall!"

The more Jake tossed out the back, the more he uncovered where they'd secured the containers they were mixing up to make a little extra on the side. They'd looked up the recipe online and weren't sure it was going to work. All they knew was how lightheaded they got when they opened the canisters and how they had to keep the van ventilated at night or it smelled like a dozen cats were having pissing contests all night.

He hated to, but he lobbed his white bag of face powder which hit the hood of the car dead center and burst like a bag of uncut cocaine. Carp had to slow down after that since he'd forgotten to refill the water in his wiper-fluid reservoir.

Ronnie took notice of this tactical advantage and swung wide at the North Y and gunned it up Jamison Mountain Highway Road 134. Ronnie knew no other squad cars would join chase given how wrapped up Leaman was with the situation and how proud Carp was. He'd be embarrassed to call for backup, so they stood a chance in this mess. But Ronnie was worried. Highway 134 was notoriously the most pothole neglected and winding road in the area and it scared him to think it might set off what was cooking and fizzing in the back.

Constable Carp was fit to be tied by now. He was worried he'd blow them up shooting with his left hand and all, but that's all he could do. He'd get up close and fire off a few rounds. Not even close to the tires. With only two rounds left in the clip he was conserving, hoping the boys would try to ditch and get tangled up in the woods in those silly outfits. But they were driving stubborn. He pressed them, tailgating and dodging lord knows what all was flying out the back and that white powder was still all over the windshield and in his eyes a little. He tapped their bumper just to let them know he was still there and planning to outlast them.

A wobbly figure with large pink floppy bunny ears, but with an American flag–striped face popped up into view through the broken windows and flipped him the bird and tossed some individual ice creams at him with a maniacal laugh. Jake had done gone and lost his mind.

Ronnie yelled back. "Jake! Jake! We're gonna ditch! I'm takin' this turn up at the bridge, but it's real sharp! Hold on, brother! Hold on!"

Jake probably didn't hear him in the chaos. The bunny-ears material was thick.

Carp rubbed the bumper again, this time by accident since ice cream was smearing over the windshield with the wipers and mixing with the white-powder streaks.

Ronnie missed swerving a bad group of potholes and hit every one of them, hardly keeping hold of the steering wheel.

Jake spun around feeling the bounces and the gravely skid, watching the suddenness of the bridge coming up fast through the front cab windows. A calm rushed over him.

"Aw, hell. We didn't even make it to Halloween."

Carp managed to anticipate what was unfolding enough to hit the brakes and skid free of the impact, but the explosion was so violent the fireball's heat swept all the way back to him and singed his left arm through his open window. The van roof peeled off like a giant can opener got ahold of it, tossing that plaster clown head more than a hundred feet into the air and across the creek into the next county, which wasn't as big of a deal as it sounds since the creek was the county borderline. They say it rolled into the creek after it landed, though, thus the story about it floating down the creek on a full moon if you catch the light just right.

And all those clown outfits? They blasted all over the place, but some of what landed in the creek was found all the way down in town for a long time. Sad souvenirs from a sad day in Labortown, especially for ice cream lovers young and old.

Little of the Eller twins was recovered it took so long for the volunteer fire department to get up the mountain. They say Carp probably took his time calling the incident in and he claimed his fire extinguisher malfunctioned. It was a hundred-year-old wooden bridge back then and it burnt up quick when they wrecked into it. The state built this new one after that and though nobody officially called it the Eller Memorial Bridge, all the kids who loved ice cream back then, and who loved the Eller clown brothers, grew up calling it that anyway.

Including me.

About Levi

"Aubree, you either get over here and get Levi away from the funeral home or I swear to God I'll call the Sheriff this time. Now I've been patient . . ."

Aubree huffed. "Fine, fine. I'll be right over. Give me a minute."

She's figured the boy was out getting into something since Levi wasn't home when she got there. The funeral home was as good a place as any to cause her a pain in the ass. It was a Monday after all.

When she pulled up alongside the Ellison & Sons Funeral Parlor, Levi was sitting on the side steps with his head resting in his hands looking pretty depressed. The funeral director, Jason, one of the Ellison brothers and an old boy Aubree dated once or twice back in school, was standing and glowering over Levi as if the kid might take off running like an escaped animal if he took his eye off him.

Jason walked over. Levi waited on the steps, defeated.

"Aubree, this is the third time!" he yelled in a controlled whisper, trying not to alarm anyone milling around at the reception of friends still going on for old man Miller. Levi had interrupted the whole gathering when he'd broken out speaking in tongues up in front of the crowd after standing in line to shake the newly widowed Mrs. Miller's hand.

"Jason, do I look like I need any more of a hard time than what I'm about to deal with at home? Now what happened?"

By the time Jason had managed to grab Levi by the collar to drag him out, the ten-year-old was already about to start laying hands on people for a good old-fashioned healing service. Jason had shushed him the best he could as the crowd giggled both of them down the aisle and out of the building despite the solemn occasion. Another minute or two and the boy would have had the whole place wrapped around his finger. Those that wouldn't have damned him, of course. Things could go both ways around here.

Everyone in town pretty much knew Levi, or at least about Levi and his "issues." And if everyone knew about Levi then they had an opinion about his single mother Aubree, too.

"Well, Aub," Jason said, calming down and slipping way back into using his old pet name for her, "if you need any help with things you just let me know now, ya hear." He'd have liked nothing more than to get a call from her, him married now or not.

A bad shiver danced down Aubree's spine. She wasn't sticking around a second longer. Old Jason was creepier than ever, especially as an undertaker.

"How's your wife, Cindy? Levi let's go!"

Jason smirked, put firmly in his place.

"Fine. I'll tell her hey for you."

Levi got in the car.

Aubree tried getting Levi to talk on the way home, annoyed with her son, but too worn out to fuss much. How many times had she been called out to get her boy from some place he was making a scene?

"Happened again, didn't it, honey?"

He nursed his usual nose bleed now, head back, finger pressing a fast-food napkin along one nostril, his voice nasally.

"Yeah."

"You couldn't just go straight home from school? Wasn't that our agreement? Straight home. Make a sandwich. Watch some TV."

"Sorry, Momma. I was almost home, but I just sorta wandered into the funeral home. I heard music. There was a big crowd today. I could hear a lot of voices in there."

"Mr. Miller was a nice man, yes, baby."

"I wish Mr. Ellison hadn't got so mad. I hate I upset him. I only wanted to help."

"I know you did. You always want to help. You do."

She stroked the hair off his damp forehead. Dabbed his nose with the napkin and checked for more fresh blood. It wasn't quite stopping.

"Lots of people need help, sweety. But they all can't get it at once. They get scared easy. Or too curious. We talked about that before coming back here to Labortown, remember?"

It would only get worse here. Aubree knew that.

She was waiting for his nose to quit, but eventually had to ask what Levi knew was coming. It always would.

"So what did you vision, Levi?"

He sighed. There it was. Her curiosity, like everyone else. He closed his eyes and squinted hard, mouth twisted up, obviously concentrating.

"Don't overdo it. We're running out of napkins."

The boy's eyes fluttered behind half-closed lids. His breath shallowed.

A hoarse whisper came from his lips.

Shomala . . . lolomo . . .

Whatever version of tongues it was, he'd acquired them about the time the visions surfaced when he was younger. He didn't look like her son at all when he transformed like this. But his voice was mostly that of her little boy, only talking about the oddest, gravest of topics sometimes.

"Mrs. Angela's hair studio is going out of business."

"No! Really?" That surprised her. That woman had everyone's hair business.

"She's worried. An ulcer's about to eat through her stomach lining. The infection might go septic, might kill her," he whispered.

Aubree felt terrible suddenly regretting the thought of having to find another place to get her hair colored.

Odjufeloshomaloa . . . flanajonlona . . .

"Mr. Turner's chewing on Oxys again. And he's about to lose his job at the Pizza Shack. His wife will leave him for it."

He could see illness. Sometimes impending deaths. Personal problems. Lay hands on people and heal them occasionally. Had his own understanding of God. All of it unpredictable.

Oddly, a lot of people mistook them for religious nuts, but they couldn't have been more wrong. Aubree just figured the Bible had been the closest thing Levi had found to speak through as a little boy, but he wasn't about saving souls and all that.

His was such a stranger thing going on.

"Mrs. Sampson's breast cancer's back."

His lips quivered. Words were trying to get out.

Shamalrajee . . . dondo . . . lofeela . . .

She had no idea what he was saying or who he was talking to or what spoke through him as these foreign words, sounds left him. It scared her at first, but now, once she got past the aggravation, "the gift" mostly fascinated her.

"Well . . ." Aubree hesitated to ask. "Did anything *happen*? While you were at the funeral home."

"I shook Mrs. Miller's hand."

"And?"

"She'd planned on killing herself by next week. She's so sad."

"And?"

"I told her Mr. Miller needed her to stay alive. For the grandchildren. She started crying a little and hugged me."

When he was finished he looked like a rag doll he was so drained. But his nose had stopped.

Rumors made for a confusing life for them both. Miserable often, hassled often. Accused, blamed, appreciated. They claimed no church, which made the communities suspicious, of course. They kept to themselves. Levi was shy at schools.

He'd been bullied, yes. That was inevitable, up until he'd quoted his worst bully's nightmares to him, scene by scene, right there in the parking lot in front of Johnny Rice's buddies who were pushing for a good after school fight. Details about ten-headed snakes with fire-tipped tails, bottomless hell pits with faceless screams in the infinite black, giant-winged math problems never to be solved in a classroom of a thousand giggling children. That was Johnny's hell.

The Rice kid was a big town preacher's son. He'd been so startled by Levi's accuracy of the terrors he'd teared up and never spoken to Levi again, which must have sent some unspoken message through the rumor mill to leave the little freakish kid alone. It worked. But someone started circulating Levi's nickname of "devil spawn" around that time, too. At least people left Levi alone.

"Don't you listen to those little turds, baby," Aubree told him when he came home so upset he could barely eat supper. "They don't know you. They don't know us at all."

"He's a scared boy, Momma," Levi told her. "His father treats him something awful. I never even bothered to mention the worst dreams, the ones with his preacher father in them. Those are the scariest. They even scared me."

He didn't tell his mother, but after a while every time they moved and he started getting bullied, he'd try this method and pretty much got the same reaction. It fascinated him how easy it was to turn the nightmares of a bully back on them.

The first time Aubree knew something was very strange about her boy had been two years before. It was his eighth birthday and she'd sent him to the corner store for some candles for his cake. A few kids from the block were coming over. He loved taking that walk.

Kids were starting to arrive a half hour later, but no Levi. The walk was only ten minutes there and back, even if he was lollygagging and chasing lizards or whatever. Ten minutes later and the kids and few parents were in the back yard having some early hits at the smiley face piñata. After asking one of the kid's mothers to watch over things she'd driven down to find him.

Early's General Store was an old timey sort of spot. The parking lot was mostly dirt. The front porch had a line of old whiskey barrels and rocking chairs. The windows still had wavy glass in most of them. Inside had an old potbelly stove where the men circled up all year and caught up on rumors and tall tales between spitting in the fire.

"Well, what do ya think that there means, little buddy?"

Aubree watched the strangeness through the rusty screen door. Levi was standing on an old Acme Dynamite caps crate, stomping his foot to a beat he usually only heard in his own ears and head. One hand open and raised, quivering toward the wooden rafters of the place, the other hand supporting what looked like a Bible from who knows where. They didn't own one.

"A full moon is blessed, a blank moon draws a devil's season when a freeze is on."

What the hell was he doing?

"A red blood moon is a time of prophesy, but be warned of

double-speaking falsities clad in the gold of greed. Of double-tonged serpents on the wind. Lies in the air."

One of the old men noticed her and slipped out like he didn't want to disturb what was happening, pulling her to the side.

"You that fella's mother?"

"Yeah. What the hell?"

"You tell us. He's been in there fifteen minutes going to town on how to stave off bleeding and flu and cow mange and milk poison. All he says inspired from the Old Testament. Y'all Pentecost?"

Aubree about looked cross-eyed at the man.

"Say what?"

"He spoke in tongues a few times. At least I think so. How old's the boy, by the way?"

She didn't answer but stormed in, accusing the old men of playing a trick on her, grabbing Levi up and telling them how awful it was to try ruining a little boy's birthday.

Levi didn't say much, just nursed a bloody nose on the way home to his party. They'd forgotten the candles.

They moved a few months later when a church approached them wanting Levi to talk one night at a weeklong revival. They thought he'd bring in a big out-of-town attendance. Another move after that and Aubree was back in Labortown, where she'd grown up.

"You need to go see Betty, honey."

"Who?"

"Betty. The psychic. On Fourteenth Street. The one with the big sign in the yard. Says psychic readings."

Aubree was confiding in her best friend Kelsey. They worked together down at the Waffle Hut. Aubree laughed out so hard at the idea of a psychic Bill down the bar looked up from his stack of pancakes.

"Sorry to wake you, Bill."

"She's no fake, Aubree. I've been there many a time. Lots of people have over the years. That's why she's still in business after so long."

"All I know is, this is driving me crazy. I don't know what to do about him, bless his heart. He can't help it, but I can't afford to move again this soon. What's she gonna tell me about Levi, being a card reader."

"She does more than read Tarot, girl. She's a seer." Kelsey leaned in closer so Bill couldn't hear. "A third-generation mountain witch I hear tell."

"Naw."

"Yes."

"Naw."

Betty stared at Levi's eyes. One. The other. Back. She squinted and focused, examining something well past his gaze. Back and back. Tilted her head to get something just right.

"Keep them eyes open for me, son."

One. The other. His eyes were near black they were so dark. Nothing like his mother's green eyes.

"Eyes that reflect back to yourself are a protection. Remember that, Levi. People won't be able to read you as much when they see themselves looking back. Puts them off."

Betty took her time examining Levi's other facial features. Rubbed his cheekbones and temples with her thumbs. Traced her fingertips along his jawline and collarbone like she was reading spiritual DNA brail. Along the bone under his eye sockets, reading his skull shape. Down the back of his head and spine. Tested the strength of his shoulders. Made him stand up straight.

Aubree took it all in, hoping she wasn't wasting their time.

It was the woman's front room, where she conducted all psychic business. And lived it looked like. Her laundry, both dirty and clean, piled and folded, was on the couch and had to be moved before they met, which hadn't instilled confidence in Aubree's opinion of Kelsey's referral for paranormal assistance. It looked like a normal place, but Betty was anything but normal.

She was a little lady, squat and on the roundish side. Her long brown hair had been going to gray for some time and was pulled up into a disheveled bun. Her reggae muumuu was flowing and festive, set off with a double-wrapped necklace of dried red beans around her neck. Silver rings, like moons, turtles, a bird skull, on almost every finger. Not your everyday Labortown citizen. Probably why Aubree hadn't seen the woman out much. She'd have remembered her.

"Y'all forgive all this housework I'm in the middle of, but it's got to be done sometime, don't it?"

She seemed terribly interested in Levi.

"I've heard of you all. Bless your hearts."

Levi didn't speak.

"You just call me Aunt Betty, alright? You ain't got a thing to worry about. We're family, don't you forget that." She rested a warm hand on his cheek. Gently.

She looked at his palms, angling her bifocals just right.

"Talented boy. Yes."

Then back at his eyes some more, over the top of her glasses.

"Very dark. Very dark. Eyes of a seer."

She laid out a six spread of Tarot cards and had Levi turn them over, explaining each one in a way that sounded too generic for Aubree's taste, talking about this one meaning fear or that one meaning change and this one signaling a crossroads and having to choose. Very generic.

But then she turned down the lights and closed the shades. Lit a tiny bit of sage and blew it over Levi's head and fanned it. He couldn't tell if he like the smell or not. She lit a white candle and handed it to him. "Hold this in this hand." She told him to relax, holding his right hand with her left. Instructed him to tell her what he saw in her. "Don't be afraid."

Levi did as he was told, not too afraid since his mother was right there in the room, and closed his eyes. Squeezed her hand. His eyes fluttered a little as usual. He mumbled some.

"That's it, sweety. Relax. What do you see?"

His lips quivered.

"Speak the words you hear inside. Don't be afraid."

Aloomaluk . . .

"Yes . . ."

. . . alanoleemik . . . eeleem . . .

Betty shook her head, wondering on the boy. He squeezed her hand harder. She winced, looking pained. The candle flame trembled.

. . . rumeel . . .

"You owe . . . Grady . . . you owe . . ." Levi began, whispering.

Betty gasped and almost pulled away. Looked up to Aubree, dumbstruck.

"You owe him rent . . . on your storage unit."

"The hell you say . . ."

"He'll take it . . . and everything in it . . . sell it."

"He's right. I'm three months past," Betty mouth in a whisper, "and all my dead husband's collectables are in there. Elgy would raise up from the dead if I lost all those Elvis collectibles."

"They had a bad fight."

"Grady's wanted it since he and Elgy were buddies. About killed each other, yes."

"Grady. He's a mean man. Be careful."

She pulled her sweating hand from his. Stared up at Aubree who was giving her an "I told you" and "what am I supposed to do now" look.

"Bless your heart, honey," Betty offered in a heartfelt tone, handing him a tissue for the little rivulet of blood slipping from his nose to his upper lip. He licked it.

"Levi, why don't you go play with the cats on the front porch for a little. Me and Aunt Betty's gonna talk a minute."

"Your boy there ain't no joke." The woman laughed to herself, seriously.

"What do I do?"

"Love him. That's all you can do. Let him grow in the ways."

"Of?"

"His gifts. Whatever they all are. These things are hard to understand when they're young. He can't understand what he can do. He's just acting on instinct at that age. Doing what comes natural."

"The tongues? What the hell's that all about?"

"That ain't tongues, baby, like religious tongues, no. That there's a guide speaking through him, probably. Native spirit more than likely. He's just repeating what he hears best he can. What he's hearing might be a language spoken ten thousand years ago for all we know. Depends on how old his guide is. Little scary, ain't it?"

"I'm more than a little scared now, yes. Is it possessing him?"

"No. No, it's just helping him express what he's seeing. Truth be told, everybody probably has a spirit guide just like it, but only a few—*a very few*—are sensitive enough to pick up on it. Half the time in churches around here when people start hoopin' and hollerin' it's probably their guides speaking through them. They just don't know it. It could be the Lord's hand on people too, but you'd think something that important would come out better understood."

"This is getting weirder and weirder."

"I'm here to help. My kind's lived around here doing this for a long time now. If you trust me, I'll help best I can."

Aubree dug in her purse making like she wanted to pay Betty for her troubles. Betty stopped her and leaned her head up close and whispered.

"You don't owe me a thing. If anything I owe you all. Didn't you notice I was wearing them heavy glasses when you come in? I quit needing them about halfway through him holding my hands, dear."

Aubree stared.

"You need to be real careful out there in the mundane world, sweetheart. You call me if you need anything. Anything at all."

Betty didn't let go of Aubree's hand yet.

"Now, here's one more last thing before you go. The hardest thing you'll hear really. If this is all I think it is, if the boy heals blood family he'll lose his gifts, plain and simple. You hear me?"

Aubree didn't answer.

"He loses the gift, everyone he's destined to help down the road won't have that help from him. Nobody. You've got to watch for that. He can heal accidently, too."

Aubree nodded.

"You've got your hands full."

Levi spent more and more time with Aunt Betty. As much as Aubree would allow without burdening her. He was too young to be apprenticed on much, Betty explained, but the company with someone who supported him and could be curious with him as his talents manifested would be essential for the young man. Betty liked the company, too. Said he was like having a young grand-boy back around. She knew he'd have questions. Then more questions. He'd learn to experiment. There were knowns and unknowns to this *inexact science of mountain witchery*—as Betty called it in whispers.

There would be mistakes along the way. Plenty. He'd be scared. Thirteen was the magic number for a young man. With a talent like his, after his thirteenth birthday there would be little stopping the boy, whatever that might look like. But for now it was a game of patience and keeping him out of society's troubling wake.

"Did you know I was going to get sick when we first met you?" Aubree asked Betty. They were at the Waffle Hut talking over coffee. Betty was out on one of her infrequent ventures into town.

"I felt something was coming. Something heavy for you. For you and the boy."

"Why hasn't he felt it?"

"His gift has trouble feeling through blood. Something about the blood connection. It's the downfall of the gift in many ways. Just like how it would all go away if he was to cure you."

"He'd be tempted if he knew."

"Sure as the world. And he'll know soon enough. He'll feel it. He'll dream it."

Ovarian cancer haunted Aubree's family line. An aunt. Her mother's mother. Who knows who else along the family tree. Now Aubree. She hadn't been right for months, feeling worn down more than usual from work. She'd snuck off to the doctor one day while Levi was at school, gone through the tests, been given the terrible news. Treatable, yes. But still. It would devastate him. Worry him to death. Tempt him.

When he caught a hint of it he'd have her good as new as quick as a word. And as much as that instant solving of her impending pain and worry might have tempted her, she wouldn't—couldn't—have any part of it. How could she let him sacrifice a potential life of good works just to cure her this single time? How selfish that would be. He was too young and immature to understand the necessary sacrifice of it. Of what the real world demanded, cruel as it felt. Cruel as it truly was.

Oh, but it was an awful temptation. Worse as the weeks wore on. And the worry. The pain sharpening. The growing anxiety of whether Levi was catching on.

"I had the strangest dream last night, Momma."

That worried Aubree.

"You were in it. And me. You were stuck up in a big tree. On a limb and wouldn't come down. And I was on the ground tossing a rope up to you but you wouldn't grab it. And it was hard to see you because the sun was shining so hard behind you, glowing red behind your whole body, glowing big. But you never would grab the rope to let yourself down. You were singing me a lullaby. Isn't that funny. And strange, too."

"It sure is, baby."

It was terrible living with the paranoia of being accidently healed. How silly of a thing to be anxious about. The sicker she felt, the more she worried about letting her guard down. She could get sloppy. When Levi had bad dreams he'd sometimes crawl into bed with Aubree. No more. He wondered why she wouldn't let him.

"You're getting too big for that now, honey. Go on back to bed." She didn't linger on hugs too long, either. Levi really suspected something the morning she overslept her alarm and moved so slowly getting him to school. Then it happened again later in the week. Late again.

That was enough for Levi to confide in Aunt Betty. He wondered what was really wrong with his mother. That's when she had a long serious talk with Levi.

Betty, in turn, had a long and serious talk with Aubree, too.

The time had come.

Walking to Betty's a few times a week after school let out was a normal thing now. A Tarot lesson occasionally. Concentration exercises. Learning crystals. Or just a snack and talking about his day at school.

He let himself in on this Tuesday afternoon. Grabbed the apple slices and peanut butter that always waited on him and plopped down on the laundry-crowded couch.

But this time something was out of place. He noticed the two tightly packed suitcases and some boxes of what was obviously toys and other items from his room at home sitting in the corner. He stopped chewing. Stared. No matter how much Aunt Betty had talked about what had to eventually happen he still wasn't ready for his mother to be gone—just like that.

A sign. His things from the house, boxed up and waiting on him. His mother gone. That's how it would happen, Betty told him. No goodbye. No chance of him accidently curing his mother in some crying fit of weakened heartbreak, afraid of never seeing his mother again.

But he could cry now, couldn't he? And he did. Like a baby, hurling himself into the couch pillows and howling like a lost animal for his momma. It was awful and all Betty could do was force herself to listen from the next room and let him get it out, wincing with each new terrible wail sent up into the confusion that was now his young lonely life.

"I hate myself!" he yelled to himself. "I hate this," he screamed. "I hate me!"

He kicked his feet into the couch and wailed.

"Oh no, Momma! Come back! Aunt Betty, I want her back!"

Betty heard that and came around the corner fast. Talking straight to the point with him was all she could manage, gripping his shoulders at arms' length, holding back her own crying for the boy. For his mother. For all of it.

"Now Levi, we talked about this, remember. You promised," she reminded him as firmly as she could. "You promised you could handle this. We've been working toward this day coming. Even I don't know where she's gone to, baby."

Levi took a breath, steadied himself best he could. Face wet from tears.

"But you don't understand," he sniffed, looking afraid now. "I've done a terrible thing. Terrible."

She held his head to her belly, hugging him in. "Surely not. You're just upset."

He looked up, seriously. He had her attention now.

"No. Really. Aunt Betty. I snuck into her room . . ."

What did he mean?

Betty gasped. "No . . . no you didn't, son. No."

"I did. I know I wasn't supposed to. We talked about it. I laid hands on her while she slept. She ain't sick no more. She'll live. Momma'll live now."

"No. No." Betty teared up. "What have you done?"

"But now. Now she's gone. I was afraid to tell you. Hoping she wouldn't leave."

Betty shook her head, disbelieving. Willing it not to be.

"I wanted to tell you. Tell Momma."

"And you give up your power, son. Give it all up just for that!" She held his face and stared into his watery eyes. She was near yelling at the boy now, still not believing what he'd revealed.

"No. I know I took a chance. But I still got it. Everything feels the same."

"No. Can't be. This never works, not that way, boy."

Levi shook his head now. Disagreeing.

"Try me!" he demanded, testing her good will. "You try me, Betty!"

How he'd called her by her name, like a grown man, showed his seriousness. She considered the situation. With Aubree gone—healed or not—and not even telling her where she'd gone, she was left with the boy to care for—gifted or not. She searched the room.

Levi's favorite canaries were chirping like crazy in their cages, aggravated by the crying and yelling. Betty glanced at them, angry, but knowing what to do. Betty stood and crossed the room to the cages and kicked one over hard.

Levi yelped out afraid for them. "Stop it! Aunt Betty!"

She picked up a cage and slammed it into the living room floor. Kicked it across the rug. The poor birds inside cackled and fluttered and bounced around, instantly shocked and near dead. Feathers flew.

Calmer than Levi expected, Betty opened the cage door and grabbed a flapping bit of yellow, pulling it out gently. She wasn't angry at all. She was crying, holding the injured animal. It was barely there.

She handed Levi the crippled canary and held her breath as his tears dried up and his face took on a more mature manner. He understood. Yes. He palmed the creature in both hands and closed his eyes. He relaxed and listened. The voices came, inside his mind, but as if the speakers were standing around him. That usual language.

Alamoree . . . sadowa . . .

But the sounds morphed. He caught a word. Another.

. . . *sadowa* . . . wing . . . *foshatooro ad* . . . blood fear . . . *katonee* . . . broken

He felt the canary's heart beating faster. Sensed its broken wing. The strained back. The lost feathers. The sheer fright coursing through the tiny creature's blood. How close to death the bird was.

Levi opened his eyes. Betty saw what was happening. Saw how fully black his eyes now were. Their shine. Levi felt the bird jump, straining in his lightly clasped fingers.

Shonodi . . . shonadi . . .

Levi lifted and opened his hands.

Heard a voice like his repeating, "Live . . . live . . ."

The New Exhilarist

"Earn Money Writing!"

How many freaking searches coughed that jolly promise up every time Sable crept toward the end of the month with the rent due and felt the sick reality of her English degree sticking its dying black tongue out at her in expectant mockery? Surely her debt-bloated degree would do her some good eventually. After a sufficient bout of romantic pain and suffering? Metaphoric starvation? In the next lifetime? Etc.?

But how long?

How long must she suffer for her art? Would success find her eventually living in her car? In a camp for writers out in the park woods?

Nearly every headline claimed a similar holy land of relief, but they were mostly the same. A bunch of generic writers earning so very little, gleaning a few bylines on generic topics so companies could ride the resulting drive-by advertising. The best thing, if you got a gig at all, was the writing practice. But writing about a new line of indestructible Japanese sushi knives, or this season's new, but barely changed smartphone, or how to better hipster style Zen color code your antique book collection, wasn't up her alley, though she could have faked it for "75 to 125 dollars, depending on realized advertising monthly traffic."

Dispirited: The Novel, her novel, already seven years old, could wait while she paid the bills. So many freakin' bills.

Sable was thirty pages down into her search and about to give in to a call for a "Top Five Old Timey Mountain Remedies for Pet Dander" article when she glanced the phrase "Write for *The Exhilarists*. Change Your Life."

Intrigued, she read on.

"Are you a writer?" *Why, yes, she was!*

"Have a desire to change your life?" *Who doesn't?*

"To change the lives of others while doing what you love?" *Is that possible?*

"Do you crave random adventure?" *Yes. Yes. Hell, yes!*

"We cater our articles to an elite clientele. We assign you field experiences. You write your blogs. We pay you. It's that simple. Do you have the interest and energy? The nerve?"

Yes! Fine, I'm interested, where do I apply?

Sable was heady with the mystery. Even as clickbait clichéd as it all obviously was.

What pulled her in was the application process: "Two hundred words. That's all we'll give you. No more. And let us add, we get hundreds of these, so make it good."

I really don't need two-hundred words. But thanks, anyway.

Until I can actually leave this dried-up town, I only escape through my pen. A little cash only goes so far, but that's not news. In my mind I go anywhere I want. But I want some real life. To get out of my head. Give it to me.

I'm a good writer and I trust my writing most of the time. I only need more of the real to write about. Again, I'm ready.

You want a writer with dangerous blind enthusiasm? A craving for changing her life? Wanting the same for others since "I've been there?" All the blanks filled in perfectly with a sarcastic spice? Someone willing to gleefully answer a mysterious add on the internet and go to work tomorrow?

Hire me. The rent's due, y'all.

She shot off the email, daydreamed about its cloak and dagger–ness a little into the next day, but had mostly forgotten about it by that weekend.

She answered a ding on her phone Saturday morning:

"I'm Richard with *The Exhilarists*."

Whoa.

"I'll be in Labortown this afternoon."

They're quick.

"I'd like to interview you if you're still interested in our position. Could we meet at the café downtown? Say, around one? I'll need to be leaving soon after we're finished. I've got other interviews in the region."

Competition?

"Does that work with for you?"

She answered yes, knowing Fanny's was the only thing passing for a café downtown.

Four hours later she was back at her apartment, at her laptop, the lights shut off, doors double locked, blinds pulled. Sable's upper lip was split but no longer bleeding. Her gums tasted of copper. She was pretty sure her left eardrum was near busted.

A chat-box rested in the lower corner of the company website, offering: *Advice on your project?*

Sable's fingers quaked trying to type through the shock of the last few hours. Her whole body hurt. She popped four ibuprofens with some leftover coffee and groaned at the screen as if someone might hear her pain.

How do you start a conversation like this?

"My interviewer robbed a bank in our town today."

There was nothing at first. Then some response.

"I'm sorry. Who is this? Who are you speaking of?"

Fucking formalities.

"Richard. The guy who interviewed me for a writing position this afternoon."

Nothing. Sure, who wouldn't be dumbstruck by this news, right?

"Yeah, so after we were done talking we walked across the street because he said he needed some cash. When we got there he robbed the damn bank with me standing next to him! What am I supposed to do about that! What sort of bullshit is this?!"

Hesitation and thinking on the other side.

"I'm sorry. We don't have a Richard on staff. Are you sure?"

What? "Yes, I'm sure! He knocked someone upside the head."

Am I? Sure?

"The man's last name?"

Sable paused. Richard's last name. Last name. She had no idea, did she? Had he mentioned it? She'd forgotten to ask, she was embarrassed to say.

She went back to the email. It was missing. The email she'd gotten setting up the whole meeting was gone from her account. She checked the trash. Spam file. Vanished. The paranoia was real now.

"I don't remember. I've been through a lot. And what do you mean he's not on staff?"

"Hmmm. Sounds like you've had a terrible day."

I don't need patronizing right now. Jeez.

"But, I do see you're on our roll of content providers, so that's good news."

Wait, what?

"You mean I'm hired?"

"Yes, seems so. As of the middle of this afternoon."

Cha-ching.

"You know, close calls just like this are very popular with our clientele. It's not something your run-of-the-mill person experiences every day. Such excitement."

"It was awful."

Hesitation.

"I'm sure it was. Are you okay?"

"I'll live." *How did she know I was injured? Or was she just being polite.*

She'd have to clean the dried blood off this keyboard later.

"It seems that's your first assignment, Sable. This terrible experience. Heck, I'd read it. It's due in three days. Eight hundred words. Put the reader in the center of your panic and fear. You'll be paid when we get it, if we're pleased with it, of course. You'll have no say over the final edit, nor will you see where the piece is published. Our clients have private access to your posts."

This is so damn strange. Is this even legal?

"That's it. Just like that?"

No answer.

The view across Main Street the next day from Fanny's gave Sable a good view for scoping out the closed bank. Yellow plastic caution tape webbed its entrance. Plainclothes investigators milled about the front and out back. A man and woman in stiff suits drank tea across the shop. She sipped her coffee, wincing when the heat touched off the pain of her split lip.

So he'd managed getting her into the bank with him, but made it look as if she was a bystander. The memory of Richard's fist glancing off her lips and teeth in the middle of the robbery nearly caused her to drop her coffee mug, but she licked the disturbed rust taste across her gums and steadied herself. He'd nearly choked her blind holding her neck from behind. She'd never seen the gun coming, smacking the side of her head. She was half out on the floor after that, but managed to take in most of the scene. Once Richard had fled on foot, she'd stumbled out of the bank with the crowd, blended in. Avoided the police as they screeched in and secured the place. Took statements.

And now she was back at the scene. Cut. Bruised. Sore. Sunglasses. Hat on. Careful, oh, so careful. In a different chair, another corner than her usual writing spot. It would only take a little while for someone who was at the bank, who talked too much, who spoke to someone who frequented Fanny's, to recognize her. They'd want to know what happened. Cause a scene.

But she couldn't worry about all that right now. There would be more bruises. More blood. Closer calls. Nosey-ass people.

She was a New Exhilarist, wasn't she?

She had a blog to write.

Rent was due.

The Work

The Reporter

From the front pew I'm able to see things almost too clearly for my tastes. *The Labor County Times* wants details, so the closer I get my shots the better the story. "Spittin' distance," the editor tells us, and at a tent revival like this, that's a literal order.

The man's collared white shirt is only worn for pride, as an example, I guess for us sinners. It's singed gray around the shoulders, and as he turns to face the other side of the congregation and then back to the twelve-person choir, I plainly see where the two-inch hole once was. It's patched up now, positioned in the center of his left shoulder blade, like a spot exactly where a killing touch from an omnipotent fingertip reached down and tapped him on the back to get his goddamned attention.

What happened got this man's attention alright. Along with all his hair. He's completely hairless up top from the lightning strike a month ago. His shirt is soaked now after an hour, heavy from sweat, easy to see through, and the pink, bubbly thickness of streaked scars shows from his shoulder blade down to his belt line.

Preacher Ed sure does love preaching hell these days. That might be my title for the piece.

"Preacher Ed Loves Preaching Hell These Days"

Sid and Nancy

Everyone wanted a slice of Ed after he'd won the lottery. I'd known him for years, but I have to admit, he'd changed alright. We were still getting along pretty good, even if he was trying to open up his own church. Talk about random. He was a yard guy, pulling his lawn mower around with his bicycle (since he'd lost his license, again, for at least the second time, not that I was really counting) on a Friday, then a hundred thousand dollars richer and shopping tricked-out scooters on Saturday (I don't think you need a license for a scooter under a certain limited speed).

He got weird, yes. But when he rented the old pawnshop store on Main and started The Church of the Holy Fire of God we all thought it had to be a big joke. A rumor. Maybe something to throw people off his new money trail.

He claimed he'd been struck by lightning up on the mountain. He'd even wear that raggedy charred shirt that caught fire when it happened. Preacher? I always thought of him as someone that really needed one. What no one wanted to talk about was who was going to inherit Labor County's arson jobs after Ed retired from doing such a good job all those years. He could burn a house down, that's for sure.

Me and Nancy had a great view of the whole thing since our tax-and-tan place was right across the street. I had my tax service in the front and Nancy ran her tanning salon out back. It was the off-season for taxes when all this happened, so I pretty much had a front-row seat for the comings and goings of Ed's so-called church.

Sue Baby

I'm helping Ed peel that nasty shirt off his body, like usual. It's heavy and dripping. I guess it smells, but I'm used to it. After a while he's sweated so much it's just water anyway.

"You want a glass of water?" I ask him.

"Yea, Sue Baby," he answers, still out of breath. His voice is hoarse from the shouting. He preached harder this morning for some reason. I can hear his asthma kicking up.

I hand him a glass of cold water from the cooler I keep stocked with ice water and he gulps it down with a few swallows, his lean neck muscles showing every move. His whole body's like that. There's not a bit of fat on him anymore.

He's sitting. I pinch his shoulder muscles and massage down deep.

"God, that's good," he calls out.

With his shirt off all the damage the lightning strike did is clear and naked. The spidery strike point at the shoulder blade. The exit point where the broken bones were once sticking out. Where they sewed and stapled him up. The river of scarring down his back parallel to his spine and well into his pants line. All of it pink and raised, almost fresh looking. Like a boiled line of skin. It made me sick the first few times I seen it.

He gives a little moan, enjoying where my hands are at, along his biceps now, deep in the tissue. I know where every good spot is.

"Do what you do, Sue Baby. That's good."

I lean behind him lower and flick my tongue across the impact scar, tasting the salty evidence of his heated work. And yes, where God touched him, too.

Ed's Curiosity

Ed typed his curiosity into the search engine.

"Winning the lottery *and* struck by lightning."

One in 2.8 trillion?

Funny. He'd have figured worse odds. The poor bastard it happened to in 1964 won a million. Ed's winnings only got him a hundred grand.

He spent the day meditating on how this skewed his odds of getting struck down, wondering if tempting God's wrath shot the odds all to hell.

He'd taken up prayer during thunderstorms up on the flattened strip mines overlooking town, his voice screaming that few feet closer to God's mercy or judgement. Either way, Ed figured he deserved what was coming, spared or struck down. Good luck. Bad luck. Indifference.

He had a favorite rock, rusty with streaks of iron. Surely standing tall on it might tempt down the mighty voice of God Almighty. So he might hear for sure what his new purpose was in this fucked-up world. So he might get some sleep finally. So the flames might leave him be.

Lord, Lord. Let the flames die down. Good Lord, let me be.

Epiphany?

When Ed came to, the rain had pretty much put the fire out. Some of his sleeves were burnt away, the shoulders and back of his shirt were smoking, there was a hole burnt where the strike hit his back. His hair was gone, half melted, half just . . . gone.

That's what he smelled as consciousness returned. That distinct scent and the mud in his mouth and nose where he'd pitched forward off his praying rock, the highest point on the strip job.

He'd taste burnt blood and mud for a week after that. And a metallic aftertaste he really never could quite shake.

Exodus 19:16 (KJV): And it came to pass on the third day in the morning, that there were thunders and lightnings, and a thick cloud upon the mount, and the voice of the trumpet exceeding loud; so all the people that was in the camp trembled.

Weather Report

Ed had taken to obsessively tracking the weather. He'd bought a weather alert radio device, one for home by the bed, and one for the truck. He felt like a spotter for the weather service, always looking up and out, seeking, which was fine since that served double-time for watching out for Jesus coming back, too. It was all connected.

Most of the weather fronts swung in from the northwest, so that's where he'd gone off into the ridges to search, finally finding an old abandoned wildcat strip mine up high, a perfect spot to get face-to-face with God.

Once he had a location where most bad weather hit first, he left his house at about the right time to arrive when storms hit that ridgeline. His best time was under seventeen minutes, and half of that was a gravel and dirt road. He could see a weather pattern on the news a day ahead of time, get a warning on a thunderstorm, make the drive, and be up there waiting for God to arrive. Ready to beg for a show of God's intention for Ed, for Ed surely hadn't figured it out for himself.

Sue Baby

I was with him when he got hit that evening.

"Come with me, Sue Baby." He didn't usually want me with him, I guess, but this time sounded different. He made me sit in the car, which wasn't a surprise. Claimed it was safer that way. I'm glad he did. Said I could smoke in the car, though he hated smoking, which was odd for an old arsonist.

He'd always gone up there by himself, but I'd been at the house when the bells on his machine went off about a tornado watch for the county. The sky past the mountains in the west were already awful looking by the time we got across Labortown and headed up the coal road. I was worried. For both of us. I wondered if this was what he was up to when I wasn't around and how many dangerous chances he was messing with all the time. It wasn't too smart to tempt fate like this, I told him. What the hell—or heaven—he was looking for up there in the storms, I couldn't tell you, even now. I really do not know.

"Nothing's happened yet, baby. Don't worry. And if it did, then I'd have my answer, wouldn't I? One way or the other."

"I think you're suicidal," I told him straight out.

"Just the opposite, Sue Baby," he swore. "I need me some answers."

The Prayer of Ed

I don't know what you want from me, Lord.

You give me this church idea and then leave me to it, like I knowed what I'm doing? What sort of God does this to his anointed? Sets them up for failure, I guess.

If you didn't want me to do something specific, why'd you give me that money for?

I've turned from starting fires to you, Lord, turned from it with all my heart, but it's so hard.

Why'd you put such an understanding of fire in my mind from when I was young, that flame in my heart I was born with? To make it that much harder to follow you? Well, it's working.

Am I to suffer it from my mind and soul, like some house burned down to nothing but embers? To let the wind come and take it off?

I come up here to get closer to you, God, but you ignore my hurt. My heart. My prayer. That ain't fair. Why hide behind the storm clouds and make all us little creatures run from you like you do? Huh?

If you got something to say, say it!

Ed's Visitor

I was in the hospital for three weeks and laid up at home for another two before I could walk on my own. Every damned thing on me hurt. It hurt to look at something. It hurt to close my eyes. It hurt to sleep. Be awake. I was out of my head with pain. Confused. They strapped me down.

A lot of the time it was just me, the TV, and the Lord. He'd just waltz right in, by the nurses' station, by people in the halls, no one noticing, into my room and have a seat by me and strike up a conversation. The first talk was enlightening.

Now do I have your attention, Ed?

I reckon, you do.

Good.

Good, I guess, too.

You ain't gonna be too well for the next few weeks, I'm afraid to tell you.

I figured as much.

I'm gonna burn the shit outta ya. From the inside out. Clean you up good. Sanctify you.

I'm afraid, Lord.

You should be. It's gonna hurt like the Devil, son.

I woke up that night from the pain. It was like someone had replaced my IV with a solution of lava. The Lord wasn't there in the room then. It was something much worse, something sent by the Lord, yes, and not a comforter. A tormentor.

This thing was leaning in the shadow of the corner of the room, sucking up light, its round-like yellow eyes drawing me into a trance.

I pissed in your IV bag, boy. You're gonna hurt all night long. Like you never imagined pain could exist. I'm gonna giggle my crooked ass off at you all night, too.

Jesus, it was right.

Sue Baby

I dragged him back to the truck best I could. He was still smoking. I thought he was dead. Would have served him fine, wouldn't it?

I was trying to flop him up in the truck bed when he groaned. "I'm still alive, Sue Baby. I'm still here." There was a bone sticking out of his back. He was bleeding. His hair was almost all gone. There was burns all over. He was damaged up all over his back and down his ass and legs. He stunk like a house fire, but with skin, too.

"Hope you feel better, you son of a bitch!" I yelled at him through the thunderclaps. I wanted to slap him right good, but he was bleeding from the eyes and ears, too. I'd wait.

Vision

I heard him in a whisper as it landed upon me at the mount. I witnessed the Lord in the flash as I fell, my eyes turned up into the flashing storm, the clouded heaven. He was like golden crystal and the lightning striking my body shot from his face and mouth, mixing with the brilliant fire that was his eyes seeing through my every thought. His arms and feet glowed bright and wide as the storm. His whispered words were like that of a million angels speaking hushed under the killing fires.

At the Chapel

The man walked into Ed's chapel like he owned the place. Ed sighed, not caring if the man heard him. He'd dreaded Jackie Phelps finally coming around.

"I've got a job for you."

"If it's of the Lord, then fine."

"It's not. It's old business. Something you owe me."

"I'm done with that now."

"You were too good at all that to quit now. I bet you can handle preachin' and burnin' at the same time, Ed."

"The only one I owe now is God."

"That's not how the boys see it. You owe me. One more burn ain't gonna offend no one."

"Not interested."

"Not asking if you're interested. I give you good money for a job you never done. What's your new little church got to say about stealin', huh?"

Ed sighed long and hard.

"Besides, need I remind you who kept the state inspectors off your back so long?"

No. Ed didn't need yet another reminder from the mayor.

Voices

It's not easy working synchronicities out. Anticipating what a human might do is near impossible. Freewill can be their blessing or their disease. Freedom. Will power. What a lovely and terrible combination.

You can liken it to gears linking up if you like, if that's the tasty oversimplified comparison your mind needs to understand the process. That's sort of like saying, *Yes, the universe is a big place, isn't it?*

Imagine those math nightmares you have sometimes. The ones with twenty-foot-tall blackboards full of chalky math formulas and you're standing up in front of the class without a clue, naked, of course, having a panic attack. Working out the necessary dominoes falling just right for synchronicity to work is something like that, but much worse. That's why we don't get it right all the time. That's what you call déjà vu. Close calls. When the math almost works, but not.

Oh, but when it does.

When it does we get our friend Ed. Preacher Ed. Well-known and talented arsonist, an everyday criminal, though a pretty nice guy all-around, born at just the right second, in just the right time and place, the era, in just the right set of influences, including the absent father and alcoholic mother, etc. (insert fiddle music on the cabin front porch and all that).

That he enjoyed spending mornings at the most successful winning lottery store in all of Kentucky was no fluke. That he was crushing on Sue Baby who worked there—that also had to be arranged, though everybody figured him and Elma would be the ones to get together. Also no fluke. There are no "flukes" in our line of work. And that he'd found enough tossed away scratch-offs to buy up some new tickets on a big winner game was sweet perfection.

But him deciding to start up his own church with that money when he might have chosen any number of limitless options, including just disappearing? That had to be Ed's own doing. There wasn't any linking up of cosmic keys to that one. That was all on him, though we were hoping awfully hard for it. I guess you could say we were intentionalizing that vision. There's nothing secret about doing that.

But when he got antsy and the time came and we had him standing on a rock and about split his ass in half with a bolt of lightning that came just short of killing him, that was some of the finest precision witchery any of us had seen in a long time.

Edification
"A lightning bolt can heat the air as much as five times hotter than the surface temperature of the sun, or about 54,000 degrees Fahrenheit (30,000 degrees Celsius). This heat causes expansion in the air as an explosion, starting a shock wave that turns into a sound wave upon reaching the human ear. Thunder travels radially in all directions from the lightning at the speed of sound, approximately 738 mph . . ." (Encyclopedia.com).

Temptation

I spent a tad extra on the thick embroidered cover we lay over the altar table. It's the prettiest thing. Red and yellow roses. A crucifix with Jesus. A crown of thorns. Gold and red trim. Sue Baby just loved it. I had it special-made from Singapore out of the most flammable materials I could research. The altar top I fashioned up thin so the fire from the cloth would eat down quick to the two sealed up gallons of gas I've hidden inside the altar. Talk about an altar call. One match and the whole place is gone in minutes.

Let's call this a backsliding arsonist's insurance policy. A weapon in case things get too weird around here and I need to bolt.

More than anything, though, there's something about having that sitting in front of me when I'm preaching. That bomb sort of lays dormant, sleeping, hibernating like a vengeful angel of God. At my disposal. No one knows fire like an arsonist does. Like I do. It fires me up. Helps me burn the word into people's heart. Am I tempted to keep on setting things? Sure. Just this month I was chomping at the bit hearing about all these Tennessee wildfires and all those acres of forest burning up and knowing someone probably did it on purpose and knowing someone was standing back watching their pretty handiwork. To smell that smoke in the air everyday was killing me.

But I resisted. By God, I held out. With that yellow-eyed thing in my ear the whole time, telling me it was God wanting me to burn the whole town down.

Interviewing

Oh, yeah, that's a good shot you got of him. Looks like you were on the front row or so. I'm surprised he didn't snatch you up and two-step with you when the spirit moved. Make sure you treat him right in that article, hear me?

Preacher Ed's a good man. Everyone's redeemable. I'd say the Lord would forgive the devil himself if he'd come crawling up to the gates of heaven proper and said they was sorry.

All I know is, I'm a saved man cause of Ed's preaching and the Church of the Holy Fire. I was killing myself. Meth more than anything. Making it. Smoking it. I was the biggest junkie there ever was. I was bound to blow myself up eventually.

He happened to have a smoke mask in his car when he saw my trailer boiling out green poison fumes. Why he had one, who knows. He knew I was either already dead or near it, but that didn't stop him, did it? No. He come in after me like God told him to. Saved me.

I was out of my head, but I do remember him praying the whole time he was dragging me by the feet out of that hellhole. It was muffled in that mask, but I know what he was saying.

Not yet, Lord. Not yet, Lord. Please, Lord, not yet.

Print it just like how I told you or don't print it at all. That's the truth.

Confrontation

"You both can kiss my ass if you're gonna use me as some spiritual rope in your tug-of-war."

They were the first to arrive. Too early for Sunday service that usually started at eleven. It was only just past nine. Ed swore he'd locked the door behind himself. But there they were. One man on the front pew to the left of him, another on the right. The voice of the left familiar, the demeanor of the right also familiar. It hadn't taken him long to figure out what was up.

Ed had been at his pulpit, studying his sermon when he'd looked up and found them sitting there in his church, staring, patient looks on their faces.

Now just calm down, Ed. By the way, how's your back healing up, the one on the left asked, sounding genuinely concerned.

You should have aimed for his head, remarked the other through a snide grin.

I'm not here to engage with you, the other reacted, but calmly.

"I'm fine."

Oh yes, he's fine. He uses those wounds now to profess your greatness, oh mighty one. To fill that collection plate, huh, Ed? Preacher Eddie. Ol' Eddie boy. El Pastor.

Don't pay any attention to the angel of sarcasm over there, Ed.

"What do you want? Either of you."

The one on the left, relaxed back in his overalls, crossed his legs, spread his arms along the back of the pew. The man was wearing gold-tipped alligator cowboy boots. A shining gold watch chain hung from his waist pocket.

There's some terrible people in this town, Ed. You know a lot of them. They know you.

Ed nodded, the list already forming up in his head.

You've run with some of them over the years. We wanted someone on the inside. Someone with an uncommon talent. Someone who knows fire, obviously. Knows the element intimately.

I like fire, the one on Ed's right piped up. *I like it a . . . lot.*

I made fire, so shut up.

"So you . . . *want* me to burn things. Is that what you're saying?"

Let's just say you have more of the work to be about than just preaching up a storm behind that bomb of a pulpit you've carpentered up. Clever job, by the way.

They deserve to die, whispered the one on the right. *So, so many of them.*

Hush now. What he means is that we can't just go around striking people down with lightning bolts all the time, he laughed. *That would be a bit too dramatic, too Thorish. Wagnerian, even, wouldn't you say. Might raise spiritual suspicion.*

Ed felt a twitch of itchy pain up his back into his shoulder blade. He winced with the memory's flash in his mind. Blinked it away.

Great heaps of them, filling the valleys to the brim. Set flaming. Beautiful.

I said hush! He gets an audience, he never shuts up. Remember that.

Fine.

But all that would lead to some suspicion, don't you think? Let's agree that a number of people need to get sent on to the great beyond—and into our care—earlier than nature might drag out. And since this town is infamous for fires in the first place, thanks to the talent, who'll suspect a few fires that took out the trash along the way?

Ed felt like a pawn between the two visitors, but then again, they struck him as if they wanted the same thing ultimately, but for different reasons.

And you're our man, giggled the one on the right. *Founding preacher of the Church of the Holy Fire of God! What irony! That is the proper use of the term irony, isn't it?*

He's the angel of irony, too. So what do you say, Ed? What's the verdict?

Ed stepped from the pulpit and over to a little desk he kept for business purposes. Grabbed a red maker and a sheet of paper from the printer and scribbled for a second, snatched up some tape and walked up the aisle between the men. He took his time.

They both wondered what he was up to.

He taped the sign on the outside of the glass:

NO SERVICES TODAY—SORRY—GOD BLESS

Ed closed and locked the door and came back. He plopped down on a step below the pulpit, burying his face in his hands for a long moment, rubbing his forehead and temples. This was where he'd prayed, on his hands and knees, in the middle of the night, alone, when things were so confusing, when he didn't know what he was supposed to do.

He counted to ten. Took in a fresh breath.

He looked up, feeling a smile work its way over his face. A real smile.

The men were gone.

But Ed still heard the voices.